Precious PROTECTED

A Lifestyle Series Book 2

SAMANTHA SCOTT

authorHOUSE®

AuthorHouse™
1663 Liberty Drive
Bloomington, IN 47403
www.authorhouse.com
Phone: 1 (800) 839-8640

Published by AuthorHouse 10/23/2018

ISBN: 978-1-5462-6367-8 (sc)
ISBN: 978-1-5462-6366-1 (e)

Library of Congress Control Number: 2018912176

Print information available on the last page.

Any people depicted in stock imagery provided by Getty Images are models,
and such images are being used for illustrative purposes only.
Certain stock imagery © Getty Images.

This book is printed on acid-free paper.

Because of the dynamic nature of the Internet, any web addresses or
links contained in this book may have changed since publication and
may no longer be valid. The views expressed in this work are solely those
of the author and do not necessarily reflect the views of the publisher,
and the publisher hereby disclaims any responsibility for them.

DEDICATION

To my family and friends, thank you all for the love, support, and cheering y'all did. This book took time but without you it would have never been done. To my readers, I am so fond of book readers you all are the best people. Enjoy this story, I wrote it for you.

MASTER

I let her go. I am broken.

It has been three months since she closed the door on my face and walked out of my life. Not a moment goes by that she doesn't leave my thoughts, she consumes my life, my heart is hers. I never thought I could love this hard, I never wanted this kind of love either. Now, I can't live without it, without her. I knew she'd be the death of me. I don't want to go on if it means doing it without her.

I had a job to do, and that was to make sure she remains safe. I will continue to do my job and protect her.

I will stop everything and anything that enters my path that keeps me from watching her. I will protect My Precious. Mark my words even if it ends my life of never having her, I know she will be safe.

I won't remain broken.

CHAPTER 1

I feel like he is everywhere. It is almost like I can smell him. I remember how he smelt, cedar chips and spice. I miss his crystal blue eyes that burned deep into my soul, but when he was hungry, full of lust, they were dark, dangerous, mysterious, and sexy as fuck. His smile made me feel safe, cherished. Fuck I miss him so much. I have picked up the phone countless times to call but I hang up before I make a devastating mistake. Before I can feel more pain, does it really matter? I am in an agony amounts of suffering.

On another note, I have been able to get my design team, I have about four people helping out. The fashion business is up and running. Doing quite successful too. I have my first fashion show with my line as one of the main fall categories. All the big fashion executives will be there, and they will choose who they want as a new line in their department stores. This will take place in a few weeks. I love designing fashion. I found an old, run down factory mill that has been for sale for years. I rent out the top floor. It was like a dream come true when I put my foot inside it. All open floor plan, brick walls, a bathroom in back, and on one 12-foot wall off to the side must have been a small kitchen. The wall has mounted cabinets and on the bottom with counter space. An open spot for a refrigerator, which I did purchase one. I placed flat tables throughout the studio. Simon, my seamstress has a table just for him with supplies of every sewing machine possible. I have a materials table, and a design table, this is where the drawings of each design is created. So, all forms of pencils, papers, erasers and measuring items are at this table. I also purchased mannequins and hanging rods on roll away wheels.

I also have my Mistress website up, yes, I created a Mistress website. I will say I had no idea what I was doing but I placed some advertising ads on other websites and before I knew it, I had two applicants immediately and then one following a week later. Brayden from Mr. Michaels office is one of them, although he has no clue it is I that is the Mistress. The others are different. Kane, I believe was in a horrible relationship and is still trying to accept and grieve. I take things very slow with him. We are working out trust issues and focusing on healing. I need to make him feel safe, wanted, loved and I believe this will take a while, but he will overcome his fears. Victor is older, wise, almost dangerous but I am in control and have him on a very long leash however, it's watched, closely. Feeling a vibration in my pocket I grab my phone.

"Hello beautiful. What do I owe this honor of you calling me?" It's my bestie, Sky.

"Well Miss kiss ass, I was wondering if I could come into town and visit you this weekend? You know I really like Minnesota and possibly may move there."

"AHHHH!" We scream together.

"Er Mer Gerd! SKY! Yes, yes you can come stay with me! Stay as long as you need too. What made you decide this?"

"First of all, stop saying er mer gerd! Second, it's just well, you are there and Jake is with Kyle so he is back and forth. I basically have dated every male walking here. So, I guess I better see what Minnesota has for me. As far as the male population."

"I couldn't be more excited. I have the perfect man to start off your spree. I can't wait!"

"I trust your gut girl, since you set up Jake I have no doubt you'll do the same for me. My boss has been kicking me around since I put in my two weeks. He's such an ass. I got to go he's buzzy me."

"Ok darling, see you this weekend."

"I'll text you when I am leaving."

I'm going to have another friend here, I say to myself as I do a little dance, a friend I can tell all my dirty secrets too. I need her. I need him, ugh, forget about him. I check my emails. Ten from Brayden, two from Victor, one attachment from Kane and nothing else from him. I read all of Brayden's emails, he is an eager boy. Always wants to please his Mistress. I, honestly, don't have that much time for him. It's like he needs a mother, which I can be, but I also wouldn't mind if my subs could be a little more masculine like I thought he was when we had our first encounter at '*his*' Manor, '*his*' being Shane. Brayden is like a little boy, I need to know more of his history, his fears so I can be a well fit Mistress for him. Victor is very smart, I can tell and a man that can hold his own. I have no idea why he is here, perhaps we need more conversation and less punishment. He likes harsh words. He enjoys when I tell him to behave badly or to strip naked and wait for me. To acknowledge is behavior, he performs this via video but he only shows himself from the neck down, he never allows me to see his face. He is a mystery, speaking of mysteries, Kane is one who I need to help and be very cautious with. I open Kane's attachment, it's a song. Before I listen to his attachment, I need to finish some projects and a new design I have for the fall line to present at the upcoming show in a couple of weeks.

Finally, I listen to Kane's song, it's 'Unsteady' by the X Ambassadors. I guess this is a warning. I try to read more into it, so I listen again, I replay the song about eight times. This poor man, he must have been hurt badly. I just need him to speak to me, trust me. I take in the fact that this is a hard limit for him. I think he is saying that he is willing to lean on me, allow me to hold him up. I just don't understand 'If you love me don't let go' we are not in here for love, this is a training site, so it must be he loved but it was not reciprocated. I completely understand. This reminds me so much of what I had, gah! I am to get these men ready for their next adventure, a new chapter in their role of Submission. I will just need to keep gaining his trust, let him feel safe, and then maybe then he will come out of hiding. I start My Mistress process. First, Victor.

Hello My Darling Boy,

I hope this evening has treated you fair. You are such a good boy for allowing Me to see another side of you. For tonight I want you to list happy times that you can remember.

This can date back from childhood or even a month ago. Now, go be a good boy and listen to Momma.

Rest well My Viscous Victor. XOXO

I receive an instant reply.

Yes, Mistress. Anything You command, is my will to please.

May You dream of me in Your arms tonight.

Your man,
Victor

He makes me laugh. He likes power but also the need to feel punished. I pray he has good memories. At times, I feel he may have had a rough childhood. Victor is easy to please me, however, he always seems to redirect questions I ask, so this I hope works. I need to know more of him, his past, his present and what he sees in the future. I thought I had enough to start with but he turns everything around. He wants the hard limits anything soft, sweet or caring he turns from. Victor, he is My man, not boy.

Brayden is an open book. Extremely easy. He is a huge softy, loves to be told he is a good boy, loves to please because he is deserving of all he does and more. He will talk of anything you ask. His childhood was a great one for him growing up, he's parents still married and love each other very much. He has never been abused nor hurt during relationships, his problem is letting out or showing his true side. He likes to submit. That takes an extremely strong, brave soul to do. He is ready I would say to find an actual Mistress for him to tend too. I think Sky would be perfect!

> *My Baby Boy,*
>
> *I couldn't be prouder of you and the way you always seem to please Me. I love that I am on your mind throughout the day. Receiving such messages from you touch the very inner part of My heart and much more. You are so good to Your Mistress. Mistress wants to reward you., I will soon want to see how it has been handy. By this you will understand by following the instructions sent with it. I have sent it via mail, allow a few days My dear. Have a pleasant night. Naughty night baby boy.*
>
> *XOXO*
> *Mistress Miranda*

Kane. My sweet baby Kane. I know nothing of, just that he has been hurt badly. How? I have no idea. I need to dig more with him. He doesn't say much and what he does say is through songs. His songs are touching, my heart breaks when I listen to them and try to figure what it is he is trying to reach out and indicate. I only guess that if I keep pacing myself with him, let him know there is not a rush on anything, he is safe with me. There is no pressure, then he will eventually open.

Good Evening Darling Kane,

I trust your day has been well. I received the attachment and apologize for responding farther behind than I would have liked too. I needed to gather reason behind the song, so I could correct or come to terms with understanding your meaning. My deepest apologies.

If you love me don't let go. I know exactly what you're expressing. You live this life thinking of this one person whom you love and you think it's reciprocated but in the end, it's not. And they let go leaving you blindsided. I am here for you Kane, I would like if you would enlighten me, perhaps start small, give Me, Your Mistress a little indication as to what happened. Is this a past relationship with another female, or does this have to do with your childhood? I will not speak of this anymore until you are ready My sweetness. I will be here for you when you need Me.

Pleasant dreams My Kane. You are in My thoughts.

XOXO

I lay in bed, rolling over I see Kane's attachment. I decide tomorrow I will respond with a song too. Maybe this is how he will be communicating for now, until he becomes ready. I look through my playlist. As I do, My precious boy, Brayden chimes in.

> *Mistress,*
>
> *i cannot express the excitement going through my body upon receiving Your gift. The anticipation is tremendous. Thank You, Mistress, thank You. i send a ton of kisses Your way, if only one day, i am to reach those pink lips to show my enduring appreciation. You will most definitely be in my dreams tonight as You are most nights.*
>
> *Your Baby Boy*
> *XOXXXXXXXXO*

I can't help but to feel warm and childish with him. He does place good into oneself, I am truly blessed that he stumbled upon my site. Going back to my playlist, searching has exhausted me as my eyelids begin to fall, slowly closing.

CHAPTER 2

Of course, a new day with new problems. I am told my fabric for the new design will not be in until after the fall show. My stress level is at its highest. I need to rethink the color for the fall line, if I don't come up with something soon we won't have anything for the show. Pulling hair out of my head, literally, I turn to my other website, Mistress Miranda.

Kane, has sent another attachment. Another song, of course, he is not ready to express verbally so a song it is. I open and listen. Here without you, by 3 doors down.

> *My sweet boy,*
>
> *I need you to be open, this will allow Me to help you. Tell Me by your words, what happened? Is it a relative? Perhaps a last relationship? To further help you I need to know just a little, it can be one word so I can understand your songs better. I personally relate to these song as a reminder of a past lover. Yes, I had fallen in love, he still is here. I can feel him, I can smell him. It hurts knowing that I will*

> *never be in his arms nor will I ever be able*
> *to talk to him. I know the pain, My darling.*
> *If you could use a word not a song, so that I*
> *know your hard and soft limit. I believe you*
> *and I will become very close My sweetheart.*
> *Take your time, there is no rush on this. I am*
> *here, always.*
>
> *Always,*
> *Mistress Miranda*

I hope that might help, but I feel it'll push him away. The song, I know he sends them because he is trying hard to speak to me. His pain runs deep, maybe the one he loved died. Please don't be that. That thought keeps running through my head, it could be possible he lost a loved one. If you think about it, the words, here without you, still in my dreams. I don't know, but I must remain hopeful. Just then I get a message, oh my god, it's from him, Kane. Nothing attached.

> *Dearest Mistress,*
>
> *A recent relationship.*
>
> *As You call me, Your sweet boy, Forever,*
>
> *Kane*

Holy shit! I got him to write words. He is beginning to trust me, this is amazing. Then another email pops up, it's Kane again but this time he has an attachment, eager I quickly open. Fuck. Another song. So, I listen. Bleed out by Imagine Dragons. "God dammit Kane!" I scream out in frustration. Slamming the computer shut, I get up and pace the room. How can I help him? I need Master to help me guide this man. But that's just it, there is no way I can reach out to him, it'll hurt too much, and these songs that Kane sends me. These are songs I could be picking out and sending to Master. If Kane and I are so much alike; why can't I help him? He misses the one he loves but what is his motive? I know mine and to help him, I need to know his.

Just as I am about to exit the building for an early lunch, I receive a message from Victor. I am guessing he has gotten his assignment that I had wanted him to do done. My stomach growls, I'll have to pass on opening his email, it could be lengthy. I hop out onto the street, take in the fall breeze and that's when I notice the figure, the figure I see a lot. I was starting to think I might be crazy but there he is, staring at me. This is creepy I can't make out who he is, I quickly turn the corner in the direction I am headed, just a small café down the street. I don't want to turn around but my curiosity gets the better of me, so I do. Nothing. Maybe I was going crazy, it could be simply that it's someone that may work in this area, hence the reason I see figures all the time.

I order a sprite and a sandwich, gather my food at the end of the counter, grab a cozy spot by the window and holy shit, there he is again. He is watching me from across the street. He doesn't hide himself but he is not in clear openness. Who is he? I discreetly raise my phone and take a picture, well best that I could with him being so far and I had to take it through a glass window. I got to distracted with my food to notice when he disappeared. Bummer, I focus hard on the man in the picture, similar features to

Mr. Michaels. Then my mind drifts of to him, I remember all the great experiences he taught me, how easy it was to be around him and most importantly be myself. Shane never judged, he always made me feel welcome and safe. That's the part I miss most, is being safe with him. I have never ever felt even remotely close to that feeling and what a feeling to have. Life doesn't exist without it, and that's all I want again, but I want it with him, with Mr. Michaels. I love him.

I am greeted by Simon back at my studio, he has a variety of colors I must go through for our fall line.

"Before I fall in love and pick one, are these available ASAP or will I be told they won't arrive until weeks after the show?" I did ask politely for I do appreciate how hard everyone is working. I have some of the best staff members, they are putting in extra time to get this new line out and ready for the show. This show is very important, one, it's my first and two, some very important people are going to be at this show. With that being said, I need to make an outstanding impression.

"Yes, Miss Miranda, I even double checked for you. I knew you were going to ask but I too wanted to be prepared. You can always count on me, sweetheart."

"I know I can Simon, I am so stressed, I can only imagine what everyone else is like. I should do something extra for everyone. Should I take them all out or a day off? No, not a day off maybe after the show. What do you think?"

Looking spaced out, "Honey, you just keep rambling on, I've got work to do."

"Simon, you shit!" slapping his shoulder playfully, "Whatever, let's find us some fall colors."

Hours later, we still haven't picked out all the colors I need.

"Go home Simon, I'll figure this out. It's late, go kiss your wife."

"Thank god, I thought you'd never let me leave," he teases me, going in for a hug. "See you tomorrow hun."

"Yep, I'll be here. Have a good night, Simon."

I walk him out and just before I lock up the door to the building, I notice him again, the figure. I quickly close the door and lock it. Only residents that live here can get in, unless you are Shane Michaels, he seems to have a key to every door. I wish, I wish he had a key to my door. I would let him in with open arms, fuck, screw open arms, I would let him in with open legs. I smile thinking of how well we fit together. Maybe I should call him. Don't do it, my one-half brain speaks to me. So, I don't. Instead, I look for a song to send Kane.

My sweet boy,

I have a song here I want you to listen to. This is how I looked at Myself after the wreckage. I am still breathing, holding my head above the storm, as much as I want to make my way back to him I know that'll be unattainable. So, I keep breathing on my own. I won't lie to you, it's hard. I look at Myself as a bad storm but there is light shining, I'd like to think it's hope, scary but it's the only way to go, and remaining positive as helped. I am here for you Kane. Allow Me in. Listen to this song.

Always,
Mistress Miranda

I sit back, satisfied with my email. I hope this will get through, maybe if I show him more of my pain he will find a way to share his or open more to the possibility of me helping him. We both need rescuing. I miss Master so much that I can feel the burn inside. I never thought anyone would honestly love me for me. I never had time to find a lover nor did I try, my life was too busy and ran by other people. I wish I could feel his skin in my hands, the softness of his kiss. I wish I could release his darkness from within and set it free, but instead he set me free. Now, all I have is his memory that twist and rips my heart. My thoughts are of him all day, I even think I am seeing him, and then I close my eyes and I can smell him. He flashes me his brilliant smile and I feel safe, but then my eyes open and reality hits. I am not safe. I don't have him either. Suddenly my computer chimes a few times.

> *Mistress Miranda,*
>
> *i have received Your gift. i couldn't be more honored to have deserved such an item and not only to appreciate this sucker of a female anatomy i will perform a video as you wish. i attached the video of me licking, sucking, passionately enjoying my naked lady sucker.*
>
> *With love*
> *Baby Brayden*

Holy Shit! I forgot about the sucker act. Oh dear, I must watch this performance. I hit play. Wow! Brayden sure knows how to use his tongue, loving his lips right now. Focusing deep on the video watching his tongue swirl between the legs of the sucker, flicking each nipple with the tip of his long snaky tongue. I'm aroused just as I hoped he would do, pressing pause I go in search for my vibrator, this video calls for releasing on my end. Hitting replay, I watch the clip again, and again, imagining he's tongue licking my spots, sucking my tits, swirling my clit. Fuck yes! A deep sigh of relief that escapes my mouth as I lay relaxed. Then something different completely happened, I bust out laughing, uncontrollably. Thinking of my reward I had given him, was purely ridiculous, but he out did himself. Sending him a female sucker to perform sexual lickings too and video it. My Brayden, is such a good boy.

Victor, however has not responded yet as to my request, perhaps this is more difficult for him to do. I also need to let Brayden know what a good boy he is. Brayden will be a great suit for Sky, she will eat him up, and he will love every part.

Good evening My dear Victor,

I hope your day has been well for you. You have been in My thoughts. Tell me, what was the highlight of your day? Was it stressful, if so let Me relax you. Imagine I am with you, I have a scotch waiting on the counter as you arrive home from your hectic work day. Kicking off your dress shoes, you see the scotch and a note. My note reads as for you to follow the rose pedals to the living room, and then proceed to the fireplace. Taking sips of your drink walking down the hall to the living space you see a form wrapped in a

> *fleece blanket lying next to the fire. Loosely unknotting your necktie, you bend over to see your Mistress cozy asleep. Unwrapping My body from the warm blanket you immediately smile, for Mistress is bare, with only the flicker of the fire to accent My form. With your free hand, you trace a finger down my spine, slightly squeezing the curve of My ass and you bring your hand back up. You sense My smile appear across My face. Pouring your drink down the curve of my back through my ass watching it flow over My taint. Then you surprisingly spread my opening and devour the warm liquid. Sending your Mistress into pure ecstasy.*

> *Always,*
> *Mistress Miranda*

Victor is a good man, he deserves my little note there. I press send and hope he enjoys. I like to please my subs when needed too in which they are deserving. I hope he replies with his lifestyle he had grown up with, I can better sense to his wanting harsh care instead of gentle. But to each his own, I guess. Now, I must let Brayden know how delighted I was with his performance.

> *What a good boy you are sweetheart.*

> *Mistress couldn't have been more pleased with your video. Tell me, did you enjoy your gift?*

Did you get off to licking the sucker while you video yourself? I did.

Always,
Mistress Miranda

Short and sweet. I want to keep them hungry, can't give too much of myself or they may get bored. I always want them to crave me, it is one thing they should want most, is me, to make me happy, to please me. Victor, my man as he so calls himself has just chimed in.

My delectable Mistress,

my do You have a way with words and imagination. i would love to come home to one such as Yourself waiting for me in the nude. i have put much consideration into your request, however i have been hesitant on delivering it. Only because I don't want to disappoint You. It is not much of an insight about me but i hope it works. i was an only child, spoiled by family. Determined young boy, that grew up successful but my success was based solely on another. i met a girl, a young lady, she messed up my life and now, here i am wanting to fulfill life for You in any way possible i can to please You, Mistress. As You know, i enjoy more roughness than tender if deserving, Mistress. There is no explanation to it, i just do.

Your man,
Victor

Victor. A true man he is. Well I guess if he has no reason to roughness than I suppose I can continue on as usual with him. Kane has been quiet tonight, I wonder if he is searching for a song to send my way. I lay back on my bed and give everything a break. I want to think of nothing, absolutely nothing. Impossible. My mind thinks of Shane. I reach for my phone, there he is, my thumb circles the call button. I don't have it in me, so I turn the phone off.

CHAPTER 3

A new day. But I wake up the same every time. The moment I open my eyes, he is not there. He then takes control of my thoughts. I shower, I think of him. I dress, I think of him. But it goes further than a thought. It's more of what he and I would being doing. He be watching me sleep or vice versa, then we'd play around in bed, and a gain in the shower. He would take care of me with kisses and soft touches. We'd dress together or at least try to dress, then eat breakfast and kiss each other off to begin our day. After a bit one of us would text the other with either a sexy remark or just a sweet 'miss you already'. So, when I say I think of him, it's deep.

"Simon, you beat me here this morning. You bad, bad man." Giving him a kiss on the cheek. I dislike pulling Simon from his family, so when he arrives before me, which is very early, it bothers me.

"I just wanted an early start on the fall show. I was looking at what some of the other designers will be entering and we have a big job cut out for us," he stares at his computer. "However, you can pull this off. I know you can."

"Honey, it's not me, it's we can pull something magical together that will shock the crowd," slapping the back of his shoulder while catching a glimpse of a design. "Holy

Shit! Are you kidding me? That is gorgeous, unique, I love it. Who is that? Tell me!" I'm starting to go crazy very early in the morning.

"That's Jacobs. You know Jacob DeMiller. This is amazingly crafted together, but we got better."

"I know what you're trying to do Simon, good job but it's not working. I'm freaking out! What are we going to do? Give me some space, I'll think of a different look. You go get some more coffee and doughnuts, I will have the perfect design when you retrieve yourself, with coffee and doughnuts."

"Sure, Miranda, but what you have is spectacular already."

"I will keep most of my designs, but I am changing one. That one, will spook the audience."

Simon leaves and I get busy to work. I pace the floor, first I decide the color, then the design. I am making this a pant suit, a simple yet elegant pant suit. Accessories will come later. I am working hard I barely notice that Simon has returned.

"Miranda, you have been busy. Geez, I should stay out of your way more often. Here, have a doughnut, this will put some energy in you. Not that this is healthy, but it'll get you going for ten minutes then put you to sleep," he laughs to himself.

"Thank you, Simon. I think I got something pretty great here. Let's put together the other colors and send then off for sizing the model." Grabbing his shoulders shaking him, "Simon! We are almost finished, well I mean close, but I think we have a home run." I am so excited for this show. My phone ringer sounds off, unknown number, I press ignore. Sorry, but if I don't know your number I'm not answering. Plus, I still need to be careful of Colin, I know he is out of jail but I don't know if he has come for me yet. After gathering the colors, Simon delivers them to our modeling agency where they find a girl to wear my design for the show. I tell Simon to go have lunch and not to return until fully recharged, we need to pull this new design together and fast. I organize the work space for when Simon returns. I too run out quickly to grab a sandwich for later. As I am walking towards the deli I feel an odd sensation burning in my back. It's eerie, a stalker feeling, I turn around and there is that man again. I am more compelled to go after him this time, he seems harmless today. So, despite my brain telling me to call the police, I turn towards the man. He stands still for a moment, then he disappears onto another street. I have lost him. It seems he is more afraid of me than I am of him. Weird. I head back to the deli, buy my sandwich and make my way to the studio. I tell Simon of my obsessive follower.

"So, what do you think Simon? Think it's a crazy man, maybe a fan that admires my work."

"Miranda, sometimes I worry about you. You need to be careful, especially if you've seen this man following you before."

"Simon, no need to worry, besides he ran from me when I went after him. And…" I was cut off.

"You went after him? What the hell are you thinking young lady? That's bloody dangerous," I begin to chuckle; his British accent is coming out the more he gets upset. "This is not funny Miranda. You know as well as anyone, the danger you are in. Please be a smart young wit and protect yourself." That last part whipped me hard, thinking Master would protect me. Once again, I go deep into thought.

"Miranda, darlin, are you listening to me?"

"Yes, sorry Simon. I will be smart next time, you are correct, he could have lead me off somewhere and well, let's not think of what could have been. Thank you, Simon," I dash my loving smile at him, he is like a father figure to me and I love him just as if he were my father.

I change the subject in hopes he can rest his mind on the fact that I have a stalker.

"By the way my friend from Illinois is coming to stay with me. She should be arriving this weekend. I am so excited to have her here, I know this guy that will be perfect for her as well. I set up my other friend, he is having a great time, so I thought I'd set her up too."

"Is this what has been distracting you? I've noticed you have been drifting off sometimes." Oh, he must be thinking when I am lost in thought of Master, or perhaps my darling boys.

"Umm, yeah. I have been planning some things for us to do, looking at job listings for her. You know just getting the studio ready," I lied. Getting back in track, "Ok, let's organize. I want the red fabric with this design, and the green with this one. Oh here, take this color and put it with the shirt and knickers outfit. We should think about shoes, and other accessories for a couple of these outfits. You know Sky maybe the perfect person for that too."

"If you want I can pull up ideas too, and then we can compare. I don't mind if she helps, that'll put pressure off you and a little off me." I can see he is getting restless.

"Simon go home. You have done plenty today, I am very pleased with what we have accomplished. I'm just going to hang around a little bit longer than call it a night myself."

"I don't like the fact that you will be here alone and then walk home alone as well. I will stay."

"Simon, no you will not. Now, go home to your family. Now!" But he didn't move. Annoyed, I packed up my things so he could drive me home. "Thanks for the ride Simon. Tell the family hello for me."

"My pleasure Miranda, now I know you are safe at home, I can rest easily. Good night Miranda." With that I shut the door and head up to my studio. First, a glass of wine, next, put feet up on coffee table and relax. I let my mind shift to the figure I saw today. I wasn't a hundred percent that I knew who the man was. Honestly, the figure did not resemble Mr. Michaels at all. Then my worst fear came to me. Colin. Was it Colin? I wonder, damn, now I won't be able to rest and relax. I decide my best distractions are my boys, so I pull up my computer, lets' see what they are doing. Ahh, my boy Brayden has something to share with his Mistress. Brayden, I will miss, he knows how to make me smile, laugh, be positive towards life. Sky better enjoy him, actually, I have no doubt she will. I open his first.

Mistress Miranda,

> *i enjoyed Your gift very much. It pleases me to know You did as well and that is why i am here, to please you only. In fact, yes, i did receive an erection from the gift you gave and the performance i gave. i was unsure*

if i could release myself, for that was not in the instructions. i did not just for You. i was miserable, Mistress. This is a feeling though that was good, You have taught me that. The very thought of granting My Mistresses demands made me feel special, not needy. So, with that said with holding my ejaculation wasn't painful but more a gift i enjoyed.

Thank you, Mistress Miranda. i hope Your day has been a pleasant one and may Your sweet head rest well tonight, if only You could lay in my arms peaceful.

With care,
Baby Brayden

Yes, I have taught him that to please others is more gratifying than pleasing oneself. My boy Brayden is a quick learner. A learning sub or to be a good sub, it is not about you, it's about fulfilling the wishes of the Dom/Mistress in which is flattering for the sub and in return will be rewarded. As I look at Victor's email, I realized I never sent him anything after he told me of his childhood. I think I have too much on my plate at the moment. I finish reading his, he sounds disappointed.

Mistress Miranda,

i hope you have had a restless day, one that has only brought joy and no harm. i hope my last message did not upset you, i know my childhood is rather boring and nothing to go off. i enjoy roughness, i hope this does not change things nor frighten You, Mistress. i shall wait to hear from my Mistress.

Your man,
Victor

I should quickly write to him. I see an attachment on Kane's message must mean he has another song for me to listen.

Dearest Victor,

I was very pleased with the response of your childhood. My days have been busy, although I trust you have been behaving? You are a good man for letting Me see the other side of you or a bit of it. Roughness does not scare me, I am glad to know this is what you like. Since, you have been so open to share personal background with Me, I am going to send you a reward. I will send it via snail mail. This shall arrive in a few days. Follow the instructions inside, I am sure this one you will enjoy.

Naughty Night My dear, Victor.

I hope that settles him for the night, I will need to reach out again in the morning. I sigh, looking at Kane's message. Lingering on it for it a bit while my finger circles the mouse just before I hit open. Holy shit, he has an actual message, he wrote actual words. This I must read.

My Dear Miranda,

After Your last message i sat back and realized this song i attached fits Us/us. i did not know You have endured so much pain, i wish nothing but to ease this from You, Mistress. It's true what the song says, i'd shelter You from the beast you are running from. i thought when my girl felt my heat and looked into My eyes that she saw the demons freeing themselves. With her, i wasn't dark, before her i was, and now without her i am once again. i can only assume we all have demons.

Forever,
Kane

Wow! He was free with her. The darkness was gone and now brought back. My darkness is here too, with Shane it was gone. Kane is right, that song does fit us. I am dumb founded and speechless. I can't believe he wrote and wrote sentences.

Sweet Kane,

I appreciate every word you have written, this allows Me a better look inside. This is how I want you to be, open. I will always be open and honest with you, you may ask anything of Me and I will give My best answer. I concur with the song, it fits us. Thank you for being you.

Always,
Mistress Miranda

Closing my computer, I remember about Brayden, I forgot to message him. Fuck it, I'll do it in the morning. I will message all my boys in the morning, for now I need sleep.

CHAPTER 4

"Is it Friday yet?" I ask Simon while resting my head down on the desk. I am moving about as fast as a snail today.

"Tomorrow, sweetheart. Miranda, you need a break from all this, go down to the café and get us both a latte and some sandwiches. I sure could use some food for energy right now too."

"I would if I had the motivation to move. I could fall asleep sitting here, it's rather comfy."

"I don't see how sitting on a wooden stool with your head resting on a wooden desk is comfy. Now get that little firm ass up and out of here before I call reinforcement."

"Who might this reinforcement be? That will make my decision," still lying restless on the desk waiting for a reply.

"I will call my youngest daughter to come hang out here all day. I will tell her that you want her to be your assistant for the day." My head quickly popped up. His youngest is adorable but exhausting. She is into everything girly, so to come here and play my assistant would be a dream for her. Except she'd be the bossy one not me. She would want to try on everything, she'd mess my designs up, it would be a nightmare.

"Alright I'll go."

"Geez my daughter isn't that bad."

"She's a disaster to a fashion designer. Cute kid but a crazy mess." Changing subject. "Latte and sandwich, any preference?" I stretch off the stool and gather my belongings.

"No, hun. Just get some fresh air, clear your thoughts and return ready to work so our weekend can be relaxing." He smiles knowing I have company coming and will not be back to work until Monday.

"Alright, alright, I am going. Be back shortly." I stop at the end of the stairs fixing the strap on my purse before walking out into the sidewalk. I look up in time to see my mysterious figure. Definitely a man, has to be. The height alone is too tall for most women, but the build isn't large. This person could be tall and lean for a man, or very tall and thin for a lady. This figure always wears a long, brown trench coat with a black trilby style hat. No facial hair but then again, I have been at a great distance every time. I watch closely through the window of the doorway. They see me, then slip away around the corner. That's when I make my way out the building to the café. With my heart beating fast, my feet hustling like they are running a marathon, my phone rings in my pocket sending me crashing to the cement sidewalk. Startled by the sound I tripped over my rushed feet. I guess you can say I looked like a girl being chased in a horror film, you know the one being followed then falls just as the killer approaches her. Good thing I wasn't being chased, or I'd be the one who dies. Gathering my stance, with a beet red face I pull my phone out unknown caller and no voice message. Once they heard my voicemail they probably thought wrong number. Reaching the café, finally I order, take a seat and relax. I want to know who the hell is my follower. It could be a stalker, or someone in competition with my line, maybe a fan. My phone buzzes this time. It's my best friend Skylar sending a text.

"Hey beautiful, I tried calling but the phone call didn't go through. I'm leaving tomorrow at 5am to miss the morning traffic out of this awful place. Can't wait to see you."

"Drive safe. I can't wait either." I text her back and hit send just as my name is being called for the order.

Making my way back to the building I notice how extra cautious I am. Looking down every alley, checking the corners of buildings. I have become a freak.

"I'm back Simon," I hear nothing. "Simon?" Shouting it louder, maybe he is in the back. It is until I spot a note on the desk.

> Sorry Miranda, the wife had an emergency.
> I needed to leave. Call if you want extra
> help. See you tomorrow, when it's Friday!
>
> X Simon

I think by extra help he means his demon. No thank you. Wise guy stating tomorrow is in fact Friday. Thank god. I eat, then hustle my ass around finishing the final touches of the designs before they are all sent off. This show will be huge for me. This could become a make or break deal. I know some big company will want my line, they have too. It's great! I am deep into my work that I barely hear the buzzer. I jog down the stairs, I notice that no one is standing out the window so I open the door. A brown box lays on the sidewalk. This box is addressed to me, Miss

Miranda Scott. Hmm, a bit nervous but also excited. I take the box inside. It's extremely light. I shake it. Nothing that sounds breakable. I open the box squinting a little hoping that it doesn't explode or something pops out at me. No, nothing like that occurs. It's a beautiful gown. Long, a soft silk, golden yellow, spaghetti straps. The chest comes to a respectful V but the back side does not. It's a V but I think others may see the tip of my crack. Yes, I mean ass crack. But omg, this is so gorgeous. I find and envelope and another box, show size and then an even smaller box. I open the envelope. My heart stopped. Yours, Shane Michaels was at the end of the letter. The letter stated:

My Precious,

Please accept my offerings. I know you must be working yourself hard and I couldn't be prouder of you My darling. I assumed you have had little time to consider your evening wear for the fashion show. I saw this gown and I immediately saw you in it. I also took in the intuitive to add shoes and accessories. Please, don't laugh, I am a man and I did the best I could. I only wanted to please you, My Precious. I do hope all is going well? Reach out when you have the time, I'd love nothing more than to hear from you.

Take care My darling.

Yours,
Shane Michaels.

I fell to the ground and cried. I cried so hard it took everything in me to breathe another breath. I quietly whispered, I love you Shane Michaels. Then cried some more. When I finally calmed myself down, I opened the box that looked like a shoe box and I stand corrected, it was shoes. Silver high heels with a thin diamond strap that over the toes and a strap diamonds as well across the ankle. The small box was exactly what he said, accessories. Diamond stud earrings, and a silver hand bag. I held his letter close to my chest. I didn't know what to do. How did he find me? What we are talking about this is Mr. Michaels, he has his ways. I miss him. Should I call him? I can't honestly accept this gift. I wish I knew how to handle this situation. I read the letter again. I cry again. I need a distraction. I call on My baby boys. There they all are waiting for me to message them. I have three new messages from Brayden, my poor baby boy I have neglected him. He will be my first. I open his messages.

> *Good Morning Mistress,*
>
> *i hope your day begins with smiles, warmth, and sunshine. i have been thinking of You and how i may please you once again. Perhaps, my fingers rubbing softly along your silky skin, i then spread kisses down Your neck to Your nipples. And then, Mistress do You wish for me to continue? Waiting patiently upon Your response.*
>
> *Baby Boy,*
> *Brayden*

Another from Brayden:

> *My Sweet loving Mistress,*
>
> *i am thinking of You and Your smile. i love my thoughts of You. A pleasing feeling goes through my body thinking of just meeting You. Maybe, someday?*
>
> *Brayden*

And his last one:

> *Mistress,*
>
> *i haven't heard from You. Are You alright? i can be of help if You need me.*
>
> *Looking forward to Your words.*
>
> *Brayden*

Shit. I have been preoccupied lately. My poor boys.

> *My sweet boy,*
>
> *Mistress is overwhelmed and in disbelief with how occupied I have been. I ask that you have faith in which you never fail to, know that you cross My mind daily. I adore you to pieces. Your messages always spread a smile across my face. You are a wonderful treat My*

dear boy. Have you been a good boy? I believe you have. I'd like for you to go out, let your hair down and see how many women you can get to smile. Return to me with the number of women, I am most positive you will not disappoint. Have a lovely evening.

Always,
Mistress Miranda

I notice Kane's email has an attachment as usual. I wish he would write more now that he knows how well it works for me to understand. I am always trying to guess what his songs mean. How one should feel with that song. And, am I right, guessing where he stands. He definitely is making my brain have a good workout. I open Kane's email. Another song, but wait…he wrote too.

My beautiful Mistress,

i am starting to come to terms You would rather i write then make sense in a song. i understand and only want the best for You. Not only the best, but to make You smile in hopes i am the best baby boy You have ever received. i did attach another song. In this song; it gives me hope. i am holding on to her, barely. i try or i want to believe she will come back to me. i may be broken and falling apart, but saying her name i find meaning, saying her name is what keeps my heart beating. So, i am holding on. i never thought i would

have this, Mistress, this pain, this love for her.
While i am dying inside for her, i have never
felt so alive. My song is Broken by Lifehouse.
i'm holding on Mistress. i am still floating
above water, barely, but i am holding on. i
miss her.

Forever,
Kane

I listen to the song as I read Kane's words. I wish I knew what made them separate. I don't want to push, he is fragile. But, damn, am I curious to why they split up. My feelings are mutual to his when thinking of Shane. I am breaking, barely breathing. What holds me together is thinking of him. I love Shane, I miss Shane. The pain is horrible but I would never regret being with him or falling for him. I listen again and read his message one more time before I reply.

My most loving boy,

I love that you also explained to Me how you
feel in relation to the song. Expressing yourself
to Me is an enormous step. I applaud you My
dear. It seems our songs flow perfectly together.
I am wondering; if I may ask. How did your
relationship end? Or is that what you need,
closure? Mine ended because he didn't want
Me. I couldn't make Him fall in love with
Me, so I left. There it is My sweet boy, Mistress
has laid more of herself bare to you. We have
a common past I feel between us. I want you

> *to feel safe in regards to Me, this is why I am*
> *here. Once W/we have established this huge*
> *factor the W/we can begin O/our next lesson.*
> *I look forward to more of your messages.*

> *Always, Mistress.*

I take a breath and relax. I really want to meet Kane in person, I feel this would perhaps be better on his behalf, instead of these back in forth messages. I will hold off on making any suggestions about meeting. I'd hate take a step back after getting him to come out as much as he has. Victor, he has received my gift, I wonder how well he did with my instructions to follow with the gift. Let's read and see.

> *My naughty clever Mistress,*

> *i found a package at my door step, Mistress. i*
> *was delighted to see i was given a flogger and*
> *with my flogger i had to use it upon myself in*
> *which hoping You were the recipient whipping*
> *me. i had much pleasure in yelling Your name*
> *to whip harder and faster. i attached pictures*
> *of my red rosy cheeks for You to see as a witness*
> *to my submission. i would love for this act to*
> *come a reality, if only. i loved the good beating*
> *i gave myself imagining it was You. i thank*
> *You for showering me with Your gift. i hope*
> *to hear from You soon, Mistress.*

> *Your man,*
> *Victor*

I smile, very pleased with his rosy bottom. I knew he would love this reward. He likes it rough, so I gave him rough. I'll leave his message as is for now. I need rest before Sky comes tomorrow. I close up shop and head home. Once I am settled in bed I open my messages particularly Kane's. I play the song as I close my eyes.

CHAPTER 5

Friday! Yes, Friday is here. What a beautiful day it is and will continue to be. Sitting up in bed I notice the gift that Shane had delivered, it's hanging in plain sight for me to stare at and become thankful yet miserable. I sink back down into bed, Friday sucks! I replayed his letter over and over in my mind. Do I call him or write back or send a donut perhaps? I'll wait and ask Sky. I love her advice even though at times it is absolutely ridiculous. I manage to pull myself out of bed, but first coffee. I continue to think of Shane. Thoughts of him are dragging, exhausting, yet beautiful and make my heart break but oddly in a good way. I love my thoughts of him. Sweet Jesus, look at the time. I quickly rush through a shower and jog, yes, I said jog down to my building. Almost there, last block and bam, I hit a brick wall, well I wish it was. Instead it was Mr. Michaels solid chest. He grabs my arm and a hand around my waist before I hit the concrete. We meet eyes, locked. Still holding me and still locked on our stare, he is the first to move. He helps me to my feet, and I feel the loss of his touch.

"In a rush Precious?" He said Precious. That stung and was hard to hear.

"Yes, I guess you can say that." My eyes can't look at him, he's so handsome. "I got your package yesterday. Thank you, the gown is beautiful, along with all of it. But Mr. Michaels."

"Please, Precious call me Shane," he says as he strokes his forefinger down my cheek. I close my eyes and lean into it. Opening my eyes, I look directly into his. He's sad also a bit of lust reflects back at me.

"Shane, as much as I love your gift, I can't accept it."

"Well, darling. I knew you were going to say that. I had it encrypted with your initials. It's non-refundable," he smirks and my belly flickered.

"You are horrible Master! I mean Shane. Thank you, I have been occupied with work lately and I had not given one thought about what to wear for the fashion show. I appreciate you looking out for me," I smile, a genuine smile because I mean it with all my heart. We stand in silence until I break it.

"Well, it was nice bumping into you, but I am indeed in a rush and shall get to work."

"Yes, of course. I'd hate to hold you up. It was very nice to run into you. You look happy," Ha! What is he looking at? I am having misery written all over my face and even more now having that I ran into him.

"Thank you," I return back. You look sexy as hell, very fuckable. I love you. Those words remained in my head though. I wish he could have read my mind, how lovely that would be or if I could read his. Even better. I go to step around him but he grabs me in for a hug.

"I miss you, Precious. Your warmth and smile around the Manor," he speaks softly into my ear. His hands wrapped at my waist. He brushes a strand of hair behind my ear. "I wish you luck with the fall show. Take care, my Precious," he pulls me in one last tight squeeze. I never want to leave this spot. I want to stay wrapped in his arms, in his strength, in his safe spot.

"I miss…" A lump started to form in my throat, I couldn't finish my sentence. So, I looked away and finished with. "You take care too," I tugged out of his grasp and quickly went to my building, without looking back. By the time I had reached my floor, the tears had fallen. Fuck! I hate this. Friday fucking sucks!

I had an hour before Simon came in. Enough time to clear the blotchy spots from crying and gather myself busy into my work.

"Hi Simon. Everything good at home? The little terror didn't destroy anything did she?" I gave a chuckle to my rudeness. After all, she is adorable, just a handful.

"Funny, Miranda. But thank you for your concerns. My wife, Lily had a bit of the stomach flu. Honestly, I am not feeling the greatest either. I don't think I should be here infecting you and our fabrics."

"Oh, holy shit! Yes, get out of here. I mean, go home rest. Get better. I'll be fine, not much to do anyways."

"I'm sorry, Miranda."

"Simon. I love you. Please go home rest. You have been a blessing to me and I will need you next week before the show. So, please get better."

"You are a sweetheart."

"Hey, I won't be long either. Sky is coming into town, so, I'll be here for a short bit longer anyways. You won't be missing out."

"Ok, dear. Have a great weekend."

"You too Simon."

Shit. Now I have plenty of time to have Shane on my mind. No distractions, it's quiet. Here come the tears. I wish I hadn't seen him. But I am also glad I did. He misses me. I miss him. I wanted to tell him but that darn lump formed in my throat. Stupid lump. I still want to do something nice for him. That was an enormous gesture for him to buy me a gown. It's just like him to know that I was too busy myself to even think about an outfit for the fall show. He is amazing. I grab my jacket, I need a muffin and latte. The moment I step out of my door I see a dark shadow standing outside the main door. To me it looks like a long trench coat. If I remember correctly, Shane was not wearing a trench coat this morning. I turn and go back into my office. What does this person want? It was probably someone for another person, not everything revolves around me. I begin to laugh. I gather myself and head back out. The dark shadow is missing or at least away from my view of the door. I head to the café.

I stare out the window of the café, I enjoy watching the people busy themselves into their mobile devises. Hardly looking up to see if they can cross the road safely, and that's when I spot him. Shane Michaels, what is he still doing in this area? I watch as he crosses the street, he turns his head my way. Then I see him being swallowed up by the dark shadow. What the fuck just happened? Is this a coincidence? Has to be. Not many people wear a dark trench coat but there is a handful out there today. So, yes, coincidence. They disappeared into the street around the building. I lost them. He was probably meeting a baby-one of his subs. I finish up at the café and head back. I just have a little left to complete my work day before the weekend starts. I'm jealous now, thinking of him and a sub after he had just held me, told me he missed me. Giving me the look of hope. Now, I'm really pissed. I put every effort I have into my work and finish my weeks jobs that need to be done. Before I know it, it's past eight PM. My phone is buzzing. Sky lit on the screen. Shit! I should get pissed more often.

"Hi Sky. Where are you?" I answer my phone completely hoping she's still far enough away for me to get home and cleaned up.

"Hey babe. I have entered Minnesota. How much longer you think, maybe 45 minutes?"

"Yep, just about give or take a few minutes. I can't wait. I have something to tell you already. I ran into Shane this morning, like, literally ran into him. It sucked big time but felt good too. I'll tell you more when you arrive."

"Oh honey. I bet that sucked, hang in there. I'll be there soon."

"Ok. I'll have the wine ready."

"Great! See you soon." We end our call and I scurry to clean things up and speed walk home. I don't dare jog. By the time I saw her car pull upon the curb, I was ready, so ready to wrap myself in her arms. That's exactly what I did. I ran out to her and flopped my body into her. Practically knocking us down but I wouldn't have cared. I was so excited to see my best friend.

"Sky! Sky! You made it! You are here!" Squeezing her tight. When I opened my eyes, I saw the figure down the street watching us! I then grabbed her things and hurried ourselves into my apartment.

"Well, hello to you and why the rush? Stop pushing me Miranda."

"I'm just so excited to tell you everything. Come on let's crack open that wine," pushing her up the stairs. I turn to look back at the figure. Gone. How do they do that? I forget about the figure watching us and grind right into my friend.

"You can take the guest room, unless you want to cuddle with me. I'm fine with that too."

"I think I'll put my things in the guest room but who knows I may want to cuddle some nights too." I can't get enough of this girl, so I hug her again.

"Let's pop open that wine. I have a bundle to tell you," I say as I pour us the wine. Sitting on the couch laughing about the good times to the now. I become sadden when she asks about Shane.

"How have you been doing honey? Have you heard from him?"

"Yes, I ran into him today, remember? It was horrible but very nice to see him. Look." I get up to grab the box he sent to my office with the gifts inside. "He sent me this knowing I'd be busy and not have time to shop for the coming fall show." I take out the dress, shoes and accessories.

"Holy shit, Miranda. Damn, it's a shame he is not a keeper. He treats you so good. My heart wants to hate him but then he goes and does this. He is a thoughtful man. Sorry, I am not trying to make things worse but this...this is amazing." As she points to the gifts.

"I know right. Even though I thanked him in person when I ran into him, I still think I should do more. What do you think?"

"What are your options?"

"I was thinking of sending him his favorite donut." I say. However, now hearing it out loud it sounds silly compared to his gift.

"Actually, I think you should call him. Just thank him one more time to show how grateful you are. Also mention how nice it was to run into him too."

"Sky, you are correct, but do you know how hard that is to do? To hear his voice, listen to his words. He drives me crazy, good crazy, an excellent crazy that breaks my heart. Then I am back at phase one."

"Honey, I know but this you must do. Trust me."

"I'm going to freeze up I know it. When should I call him? Now? Wait, let me practice on you first."

"Sure. I'm Mr. McHottie Michaels what are you going to say to me?" I can't take her seriously, I begin laughing.

"Agh! I can't. I'll just call him and wing it."

"Yes, you can, and you will. Good luck hun, I'll go unpack so you can have privacy," she gets up from the couch heading to her room.

"We both know you will be listening in, nosy girl."

"Of course, I wouldn't miss it for the world."

I feel my hands shake holding the phone. I scroll down to his name. Master. On the first ring, he answers.

"Precious, amazing timing. I too was just thinking of you. We are in sync too often it's uncanny how much our minds are alike. What do I owe this pleasure? Are you ok?"

"Yes, Master. I mean Mr. Michaels. I just wanted to thank you again for the gift. Really you shouldn't have but I absolutely love the gesture. I hadn't given a thought to my evening wear for that night and now it is lifted off my shoulders thanks to you. Again, thank you so much from the bottom of my heart."

"Precious, you know I would do anything for you. If it places a smile for just a moment upon your beautiful face, I would do anything." A long silent pause between us both. It seemed forever until the silence was broken. "Precious? Are you alright?" He adds.

"Yes, I am. Thank you for asking. I have been up to my elbows with fabric and designs. I can't wait for all this to be over. I love being busy, it's a distraction to life but the stress can go away."

"Distraction? What distraction is it you wish gone, Precious?" Oh shit, I did say that didn't I.

"All I meant is that it is nice to have something to do. I like keeping busy that's all."

"I know when you are lying to me Precious. Remember I am here always for you."

"I know and I appreciate that so much. I also want to add how lovely it was to see you again. I miss you too. I liked the way I was with you. How you allowed me to be me and have decisions of my own."

"I'd give you the world Precious. All you need to do is ask for it and I'm yours." I hate when he speaks in such manner. I don't understand and he hurts me when he says such nonsense. He will never be just mine, he doesn't do that. "I adore you Precious, running into you was the best gift in months for me. How is your Mistress site handling?" Still thinking about his last sentence, giving me the world if I ask for it. "Precious?"

"Yes, Master. I am here, sorry. The Mistress site is great, I am still learning as I go. I have three subs. I call them my sweet boys. It's fun, but I have one that I am still trying to figure out. However, he reminds me so much of our relationship and it ending rather rapid. He is struggling, so I am patient."

"Good girl Precious. You'll do just fine and you will end up healing him. He landed himself the best person to work with, and that is you."

"Thank you Master, but don't forget I did learn from the best. I guess I should head out. I just wanted to thank you, truly, it means so much to me your gift."

"My darling no need to thank me, you mean that much to me. I wish you a pleasant evening. Take care, Precious."

"You too, Master." Ahh, I meant to say Mr. Michaels but Master is so natural to me, so I left it at that. I place the phone down and immediately chug the bottle of wine.

"SKYYYYYY!" I shout for her.

"Yes, I am here honey. I am here," now in tears, she holds me as she takes the bottle from my hands. "Tell me. What happened?"

"I fell in love with him, that's what happened. Fuck! The things he says. I don't understand him."

"Like what? What did he say?

"I'd give you the world just ask for it and I am yours. Or you mean that much to me. Running into me was the best gift he's had in months. In months, Sky. Get it, it's been months since I've seen him." I fall back all dramatic onto the other end of the couch. "What the fuck does all that mean? What is he saying? I'd like to know please. Because if he is saying what a normal person says to someone when they're in love with them then I get it. But he doesn't do love, so what does his words mean?" Sky sat silent while I went on

46

my rampage. I continued to do so for quite some time until I looked up at her. "Well?"

"Settle down, Miranda. I'm sorry but please let me laugh for a moment."

"Oh great, you find this humorous?"

"Well, yes I do. Look at you. You have never had this before. You were never able to experience this kind of drama, or have a life for yourself because others were running it. So, I do find this a bit funny, but most definitely not at your pain."

"I can appreciate that. I need to get him out of my head, don't I? Perhaps even my heart."

"Oh honey. I don't think so. What I get out of this is he is trying to tell you he wants you and only you, Miranda. If you listen to him, he is trying to reach out. Remember he has never done this before you know a 'relationship' but to my eyes he is doing even better than what the normal man would do. I guess if I were you I would remain in contact quiet often with him. Go out to lunch, catch some coffee together. Maybe just call him occasionally, or a text that you are thinking of him. Miranda, I believe he loves you and he is in pain more than you even."

"Are you serious Sky? So, what if I do that and he has no interest in me what so ever. Then, I will die. I'm already almost dead because of him. I don't think I should continue on with him, it's just too hard. I love your possibility, your drive of hope for the two of us, but I'm not there with you. I need to let go."

"You will never know if you don't risk it." I knew she was going to say that, and she is right. 'What if' will always hang over my shoulder. I will regret not giving it a try. Ok, I will do it.

"I'm going to call him back and ask if he would like to meet tomorrow for a quick coffee in the morning. This way, I am sure you will still be sleeping and then I can go meet him and try to woo him."

"Woo him? And how will you do that?" Sky looks amused that bitch.

"Well, I will buy him his favorite donut with his coffee. It'll be a cute, simple gesture. One he will most definitely take notice on and adore." I pick up my phone, then pause. "This isn't cheesy is it? I mean calling him again?" Second guessing my decision to call him.

"Call him, now!" Sky knows I am rethinking my thoughts.

"Precious, once again, I am honored with your grace. I am a lucky man tonight," I can feel his smirk behind that comment.

"I was just wondering if you wanted to meet for coffee tomorrow? I was thinking around 8am at Struddles." Squeezing Sky's hand, praying he will.

"I would love to Precious. Thank you for the invitation."

"You are more than welcome, Master. I will see you in the morning."

"Can't wait, Precious. Have a pleasant night, darling."

I hang up the phone and begin jumping up and down. Sky joins in on the jumping and screaming. I feel like this is my first date with my first crush. I have butterflies. I love this feeling. Then I think about my baby boys. I should check in with them. I am too excited right now. Sky and I drink, laugh, and talk throughout the night. Finally, closing my eyes very late into the dark hours. I dream of my Master.

CHAPTER 6

Saturday morning couldn't have come fast enough. I rise out of bed with the biggest smile, knowing I am only hours away from meeting Shane. I grab my computer, I need to make time for my subs, my babies. I sign in and see that Kane and Brayden have left me a message. I didn't see anything from Victor. I must reply to him first. Awe, yes, he is waiting for me to describe how much I have enjoyed his beating. Well it's him beating himself and the pictures of his rosy cheeks. Oh, mer gerd! I look around to see if Sky heard that. I know she's in the other room, but she cannot stand when I say er mer gerd. I don't know why when it is so much better than oh my god, am I right? I look at his behind again, not bad at all. I think to myself.

Dearest Victor,

I couldn't be more pleased with you and how well you handle the flogger, especially on yourself. I am extremely grateful that you took special care to the toy and your needs. Hoping it was Me smacking your ass. The evidence was very helpful, Mistress Miranda is very

> *proud of you. I hope this has found you well*
> *and that your ass has gone back to its regular*
> *color. I want you to have a pleasant weekend.*
> *On Monday, report to Me the adventures you*
> *took and what you liked best.*
>
> *Happy Journeys,*
> *Mistress Miranda*

That was easy, quick, and next. Kane. I see an attachment, gersh, I hope not again. I open his email. Damn it! Another song attachment.

> *Mistress Miranda,*
>
> *i apologize i have no words for You today.*
> *i haven't come to terms that it's over.*
> *Therefore, i don't need closure...yet. Please*
> *just understand, i need her.*
>
> *Forever,*
> *Kane*

I listen to the song, Believer by Imagine Dragons. So, he is still holding onto hope. He isn't ready to through in the towel, nor call his relationship over. I am at a complete loss with him. But, like him, I am holding on to it too, holding on to hope. I wonder if he communicates with her. I'll wait until I can understand better what it is I want to write to him. Brayden what have you got for me.

My beautiful Mistress,

i did as You asked. i went out and flirted, gave compliments, made women feel great. i got a total of 56 amazing smiles. i love making women feel beautiful it is such a blessing when You can see how genuine they are after making them feel honored. i had fun with this assignment Mistress. i wish to know; do i make You smile?

Baby boy Brayden

My sweet Boy,

Of course, you always bring a smile to My face. You have a way of doing so every time I read your messages. I am very pleased and let's say impressed. Fifty-six smiles, wow. I must be doing My job correct for you to feel such power over pleasing a female. you are one of a kind baby boy. I have something I wish to give you however, I need a little more time before this happens. Enjoy your weekend and I will be in touch on Monday.

Always,
Mistress

I need to write to Kane, but what? I struggle to much over thinking what I should write. I want my message to explain to its very depth how I need him to express through words. I do love and enjoy the songs. I find it romantic, artistic but I also find him hiding behind the music. I listen to the song again fishing for clues, a possible statement he is trying to make. One, he is in pain. Two, lives in a cloud of believing. Three has lived his particular life but needs her in it. Fuck I don't know.

> *Dear Kane,*
>
> *My brain scatters thinking or trying to make out what it is your saying, describing. Perhaps you should just reach out to this girl. You clearly need closure or clarity on her standing point. I may need to let you go, I hate to say this because I truly want to help you. However, I believe you are not ready for help, you need to time to yourself for reflection and healing. This is not a goodbye, I have not made My decision quiet yet. Please reach out to her, you need this. My heart lies heavy for you My dear Kane. Would you like to meet?*
>
> *Always,*
> *Miranda*

After pressing send I regretted my comment on letting him go. In all honesty, it is best he seeks her out, he is completely broken more so than I am. Which reminds me, I get to see my man in an hour. My chest fills with warmth, my face brightens as a smile spreads wide across. I love how Shane makes me feel.

I go through everything in my closet. Stressed at what to wear I scream for sky.

"Sky! I need help." Nothing. I hear nothing, no one rushing to my aide, what good is she. I go to her then. Opening her door, she sleeps peacefully but not for long. I jump on her bed, get right in her face. "Sky!" I shout.

"What?" She mumbles.

"I need help. Get up."

"If this is how my weekends are going to be, I am finding a new place to live." She threatens me.

"How dare you. I am in need of drier help and you threaten me. Rude. Now get up, we need to find something to wear and then you can go back to bed." I struggle pulling her out of bed.

"Miranda, just bring me some items and I'll put it together." I quickly gather outfits and throw them at her.

"Gee thanks." She says as she sits up looking things over. "Coffee, right?" She asks.

"Yes."

Grabs a pair of dark blue skinny jeans and a maroon long sleeve V-neck shirt and throws them back at me.

"And you're the fashion designer." She moans, then she plops back down in bed.

"Thanks Sky." I run out, make my hair and face look presentable but not flashy as if I am trying too hard. Shane likes me simple, natural, so that's what he will get.

My knees are weak, my hands shaking and sweaty. I am so nervous walking to the coffee shop. I spot him as I turn the corner, he smiles as his eyes hit directly to mine. Damn he is a tall drink of water. He grew his hair a bit longer. Short on the side but longer on top and his goatee is now formed into a beard, a short beard but looks perfect on him. It's kind of like young sexy bachelor meets powerful handsome business man. He waits for me at the coffee door. My stomach turns the closer I get, I feel my face heat up. Shane bends to kiss my cheek and stupid me turns to kiss him. Yes, I kissed him on the lips. If I said my face was heated now it's definitely steaming red hot flames. I couldn't look him in the eyes after that, oddly though as I look off to the side I see my trench coat stalker. I quickly draw my attention back to Shane.

Shane smiles, "That was a pleasant surprise. One very much missed." He turns opening the door holding his hand out gesturing I lead. Everything is so easy with him, I am not told what to do or what I can eat. We order our coffee and split a donut. His favorite of course. A long John custard filled with chocolate frosting on the top. Yummy, they are excellent. He finds us a table, pulls out my chair. True gentleman, I lean in to him so I can soak up his delicious smell. I love the way he smells.

"You approve?" He asks. I believe I just got busted.

"Sorry, I always loved the way you smelt. And yes, I approve."

"Good, so I don't need to go change then." He smirks. I blush.

"You would go change if I didn't approve?"

"Of course. I want nothing but to please you darling and if I need to change my after shave then I would. For you, anything."

"Shane, I..." He cuts me off.

"I'm sorry Miranda. Let's just enjoy our morning and the company we are with."

"I completely agree. I have fallen in love with your donut though. I never have been introduced to a delicious piece of sweets. Now I can't get enough of it." I look at him just as he opens his mouth to speak then closes it just as fast. I wonder what he was going to say.

"Should I order another since you love it so much?" He teases. I look down to his half. "You may have mine if that's what you want." Looking directly into my eyes though it feels he is searching deeper. I grab his half of the donut and take one bite then return it back to his plate.

"The fashion show is next week. I am overwhelmed, terrified, yet extremely excited. I hope my line does well. Honestly, I hope I get a contract with a big wig, you know." He's thinking. I wonder what is going through that marvelous brain of his. I almost want to reach over the table, pull his face to mine and kiss him hard one more time. I want him to remember me for this feels like it may be the last time I see him. We definitely are not in his part of the city and his demeanor if off today. It is like he needs to inform me, he's hiding information I can tell by how he drifts off. It's like he is deciding how to tell me, choosing his words wisely.

"Shane, is there something you need to tell me? You keep giving a concern expression. Is everything alright with you?" I touch his hand only I hold it longer.

"Precious, may I call you Precious?" I nod yes with a smile. I love nothing else for him to call me but maybe 'his'. "I know I said let's enjoy our company and not to go deep but I need to. I love this. Us. Sitting here talking. I miss you, I genuinely mean that. I hope in the future you continue to want to meet or speak to me."

"Are you trying to tell me you need to take off already?" I tease.

"Well, I do have business to take care of, but I have a few minutes before I need to rush off."

"Please, don't let me hold you back." I swallow the lump forming in my throat, fuck I feel the tears coming. I turn to look out the window and there he is, my trench coat stalker, watching. "I wish we had longer too, but I should return back as well. Sky is here visiting, actually, she's moving here." I tell him. He raises an eyebrow, as if he is interested and wants me to continue but then he stands placing himself next to my chair, holding a hand out to help me up, I take it. I fall into his arms. I don't want to leave, not so soon we just sat down but it can't be like this. I should have never done this, meet him. I need to get it in my head that he does not want me for more than anything else but just as we were, fuck mates, perhaps. I don't even know what we were. He at the very least does wrap his arms around me for the hug. We walk out together, then depart different ways. I couldn't look back, I forced myself not too as the tears fell. I knew this was it, the last time I was going to connect with him. It just hurts too much. I feel sharp shreds of thin pins rip through my heart. A tornado swept through my stomach, I became nauseas. A stream of tears fell fast. I didn't want to go home, I needed air, space, plus I couldn't face Sky so soon. I decided to go for a walk instead. My brain is scattered, I feel lost all over again, I hate pain, especially beautiful pain. I take my phone out of my pocket. My boys, my sweet boys, now is when I need them the most. I skip over Victor and Brayden, go straight to Kane. He is my best distraction. I see no attachment. I hope this is good and more than one or two words.

Mistress Miranda,

i went absolutely blind after reading your message. i don't want you to leave me, i need help yes this I know. But i need help from You. W/we can help each other. i know You are in pain just as much as i am. i don't want You to feel as if You have not done Your job, You have. i am talking and releasing my pain, my heart aches. i have been able to go back to work, i actually look up when i walk now. Before, my life was dark but content. Then she entered my soul and life was brighter, she made sense, she was my sense to understand. All i wanted was to make her mine and i let her go. i am the fool not her. You are helping me see this and i know i need to see her, but i am terrified of being rejected. i would like to wait before i make that jump and call her. i would love to meet with You as well Mistress but, i need more time. Please continue to devote Your time to me. i look forward to Your words of wisdom. You are my healer, Mistress. i need You.

Forever,
Kane

My heart broke for the second time today, but this break was a happy break. I have helped him come out of his shell. He needs me and that is all I needed to hear. I will continue to help him he made that decision for me. Brayden has left a message as well, but first, I will message Kane.

>*Dearest Kane,*
>
>*I was very touched on your last message. I will continue to help you heal. I am pleased to know that I have assisted in some form with the road we travel on and the detours we take. I most surely can wait to meet, only when you are ready My dear. I have had many bumps and curves that I have come across in life too, but these longer rides help on different levels. They allow me to dig deeper and realize a situation before jumping on it. I believe I need you too.*
>
>*Always,*
>*Mistress Miranda*

I hope that will give Kane ease, it did for me. I look at Brayden's, I hesitate before opening only because I think he is ready, ready to be let go. How ironic. Letting go is the subject of the day. I open it.

>*Sweet Mistress Miranda,*
>
>*i can't be more curious as to your words of You having something for me but need more time.*

Please Mistress, can You explain more to me.
Have i been bad, i do only wish to please You.
i have faults this i know but what have i done
wrong? Can we meet in person soon, i really
can do more for You if You allow me to be of
Your presence? As You can see i am having a
meltdown.

Your baby boy,
Brayden

Oh, my dear boy, I have gotten him all flustered. Damn, he is adorable. Sky better treat him well. However, I have no worries, he will ruin her. I can see her now, her tough exterior but she will become mush once he captivates her mind, soul, and body. I better reply to him before he does have a meltdown.

Dear baby boy,

Mistress is not one bit disappointed in you. I
have a little something for you a great treasure
I must say. I have been very proud of you and
the way you tend to Your Mistress. I would
love to meet in person very soon. I will keep
you updated.

Always,
Mistress Miranda

That should leave him with some peace of mind. Hopefully. Looking up from my phone I see my trench coat stalker, this time I make my way towards them. Nervous they begin to back up. Then they are gone. What the fuck? I need to figure this shit out, why the hell do I have this person following me? I start heading back home, time to face reality and Sky with all her questions. The moment I enter Sky is on top of me.

"Well it's about time. I almost called the cops thinking you were kidnapped. Or wishing he kidnapped you is more like it." She winks at me. "So how did it go? Tell me everything."

"Honestly, it sucked." And the tears came out forcefully. "I hate this Sky. I can't see him again, he doesn't want anything to do with me. We sat down then he is up saying he needs to go. I didn't even get to say much." I continue to sob, grabbing a Kleenex to wipe my snot.

"Mother fucker!" Sky says angry. "What the hell? Who does he think he is? I'm going to kick his Master fucking ass!" She continues on, however that did make me chuckle.

"Oh, Sky I love you." As I dry off my face. The tears have seemed to subside for now.

"So why did it take you so long to come back home?" She asks.

"I went for a walk. I needed to think about things, you know talk myself into letting go. But I don't want too, I want to stay wrapped in his arms forever. I want to call him mine and he call me his."

"Sweetheart I am sorry you are going through this. Do you want to go have a girl's day?" She winks at me and that means trouble. Sky is always trouble.

"I'd love too. I'm also very hungry, let's go grab lunch and head over to the spa, then shopping after and then go out meet some men, real men who want to be in a relationship. Ones that want to love you and never leave you. Ones that…"

"I get it honey. Men that will stay and be our forever. I get it. We can go find our forever's." Sky soft spoken and understanding stats. I give her a big hug.

"Ok. Let's go!" I couldn't get my morning event with Shane out of my head though, I hide that from Sky. She never brought it up so I can only guess I did a good job disguising my thoughts or she was better at pretending not to notice.

CHAPTER 7

After a wonderful girl day, we are now going to make it an even more exciting girl night out. Shane never left my thoughts during the day and I know he will continue to burn through my mind tonight. *How will I find my forever if he is all I want?* So, maybe tonight I will just have fun, enjoy my time out, just not look for my future man at least just not yet.

Sky is dressed in a mini skirt, with a sequence black tank top with tan high platform sandals. Her thick hair lays beautiful flowing below her shoulders. I have on tight black leather pants with a tiny white top, I am wearing black high heels which adds to my already tall enough height. My hair is short so I just mess with it a bit make look like I was well fucked. It's time to rock 'n roll.

Taking an Uber to the club was Sky's idea, I'm beginning to regret this whole night already the moment we pull up to the curb. The music can be heard from outside, it looks dark, hardly lit. I just have this horrible feeling creeping inside my stomach. We are immediately escorted into the club, of course women are let in especially if you are wearing a mini skirt and look like Sky. Once inside it's even louder and darker. The lights are a red pink color so everything is colored to the lights. I have been offered drinks already that I've had to deny. Sky isn't taking any offers either. This just may be an early night. Until a very attractive man spies Sky and she him. I find a small table to sit at as I sip on my drink. A fruity cocktail that isn't really hitting the spot. I twirl the umbrella decoration that probably was part of the cost of the drink. He must have noticed how bored I am when I hear a deep voice say,

"Not going so well for you tonight? Bad day, thought going out would have helped, but you then realized, this truly sucks?" I look up and chuckle, how spot on this man is.

"Are you a mind reader? That is exactly how my day went, horse shit and thinking going out would have solved all the problems but now it is only gathering more." He takes a seat as if me returning a response was an invitation.

"I wish is was a mind reader then I would know what goes on in those beautiful minds you women carry. However, I am in the same boat as you. Bloody hell day, my night is looking to be the same." Suddenly I like this guy and his accent is totally cool. We begin to order shots for every horrible thing that happened in our day. Then we turned it into every horrible thing that has happened in our life. Let's just say it was a fuck load of shots. By the time I call all shots off it's too late for me. I am more than half in the saddle, I try to find Sky as I sit at the table with this stranger who is calling an Uber for himself, he thanked me for a helpful night of laughter but yet for an awful morning of a hangover to come. I continued to search for Sky through the crowd and that when I saw him, Colin. At least I thought I did I'm not sure, I'm drunk. The room is beginning to spin so I text Sky.

Sky, come quick! I think he is here!

I receive a text back almost immediately.

Where are you?

At a table by the bar.

What bar are you at?

The same one as you! Hurry, He keeps staring at me!

Who is he?

Colin!!! Sky come quick!

On my way Precious don't move.

Precious? Sky doesn't call me Precious. I look closely at my phone, sweet Jesus fuck! I texted Shane. Panicking, I look up in the direction where I thought I saw Colin. He isn't there anymore. I quickly text Shane back.

I'm sorry I thought I was texting Sky, she is here with me no need to come Master. Colin isn't here I am drunk and saw someone that looked like him. Please don't come.

I feel my phone vibrate as I am pulling Sky out of the club now. We grab a cab outside as I hold my tears in. Pulling from the curb I see Shane running inside the club.

I go to yell his name when I realize the window is up. My phone vibrates, I know it is him. It continues to vibrate, finally I look at it.

Where are you Precious?

Precious, answer me.

Precious, Please, I…

Fuck! I can't take it, tears fall as I begin to text back.

I found Sky and we left the club. Going home.

My phone vibrates again. I don't have the urge to look at it so Sky does.
"He wants to come see you, make sure you are alright." I don't answer her. "Miranda, he cares."
"No. I don't want him over."
She texts him back.

Hi this is Sky, she is fine. No need to come over I will put her to bed and have her call you tomorrow.

Please have her call Me tomorrow.

"He says to call him tomorrow, Miranda. Do you want me to respond?"
"No, just hang up now."

I need help out of the cab and up to our apartment. As I hit the pillow I feel my phone hit the bed next to me. I pass out moments after.

Morning hangovers are the worst.

"Fuck! Sky, it's noon already. I am so sorry, your first night here and I am a complete wreck. Promise I'll make it up to you." I hear feet shuffling down the hall. The door to my room cracks open. There he stands in my door way, tall, handsome, with a glass of orange juice and pills for my headache.

"Shane. Hi." I feel like shit. I look like shit. Now here stands the man I love.

"I called you this morning. In fact, so much that Sky, your friend answered and told me to come over. She had errands to run." He looks down uncertain if he should be here, maybe even regretting it. He walks into the room more, hands me the glass and pills.

"Thank you." I say as I sit up and take the glass. "I would have called you later you know." I say.

"Do you think so? I don't see you doing that, honestly Miranda. You have been avoiding me and you never do as ask. So, there is my reason."

"Did you come here to scold me? If so please leave, I don't need this right now." I look up at him. He doesn't know what to do, stay or leave as I had asked him to do.

"I'm staying. You can't get rid of me that rapid, Miranda." His voice stating my name is piercing. "We need to talk."

"Can it wait?"

"No."

"Fine. What?"

"Last night you said 'he is here' who is he?" I need to replay last night's events. Colin.

"I don't remember I was petty under the influence. I met a guy who had just as bad of day as mine so we took shots for everything bad in our lives." I realize after saying that my night sounded ridiculous.

"Do you have any idea how dangerous that could have been? Given you were alone and with a complete stranger…" I cut him off.

"Stop. Just stop. I know but I have reason and since when did you care?"

"I care very much for your well-being. I only want you safe and happy."

"What makes you think I am not?"

"I don't. I know you are doing well and are content with your work and website. I am concerned for your safety however."

"You can stop stressing over it, I am fine." He drags his hand through his hair, there's more he wants to say but doesn't.

"Are you feeling better? I suppose I should leave now." He stares deep into my eyes. Like he is waiting for me to say stay. He never told me to stay so why should I when we both know he isn't truly going to stay. Forever.

"Yes, I am better, thank you. You are free to go Shane. I can manage my day from here on."

"Yes, very well. I do have work to attend to. It was nice to see you even under the circumstances. It's always a pleasure to see you, Miranda." He bends down kisses my forehead and turns to leave. Once I hear the front door close

I let the tears fall. I lay in bed for a while until I fall asleep for the second time.

I am woken up to Sky screaming in the other room. Now I hear a crash. *What the hell is going on out there?* I try to roll out of bed, the accomplishment is successful. As I walk like a zombie down the hallway to Sky, I hear another violent crash.

"Sky? What the hell?" I say shrugging my shoulders.

"Ahh! Sorry Miranda but I am pissed because Dexter here," she points to the tv, "is a killer and the other bad guy killed his wife."

"That is what's causing the commotion out here?"

"Well, I kind of like Dexter," she says uncertain what my perception may be.

"You like a killer? Nice Sky, just don't be bringing him home, here."

She throws a pillow at me, "I knew you'd make fun of me!" I turn back to my room laughing.

I grab my computer realizing I have not been in contact with my sweet baby boys.

Mistress Miranda you have 5 messages. I decided who to open first, Victor, Brayden, or Kane. I go with Victor.

Mistress Miranda,

> *i know the weekend is not over but since i am sitting here watching Top Gun I thought i'd write. My Friday was nothing but working late. i enjoy my job so that does not bother me to do so. Saturday, i met an old friend out at a bar, he was surprised it seemed that i was in*

the area, but it went pleasantly well our time out. Today i shall stay humble and watch the tube. i will wait for the Vikings football game. My favorite part of my weekend is this, just sitting on the couch relaxing. What would make it better is if you Mistress were by my side. Is there going to be a day we meet? Are you going to continue to be my Mistress in real life? i would love nothing more than to have You in my grasps at all times. i hope Your weekend was as lovely as You. i will be looking forward to Your reply.

Your man,
victor

Oh Victor, he is a handful. What is it with these guys wanting to meet. I thought I was clear in the contract online training, no real-life training. However, I did tell Brayden I'd meet him only because I am introducing him to his next real-life Lady. Little does Sky know this, but she'll love it and him, this I am positive. As far as Kane, I think I would have a better feel of his situation if I can just meet and chat in person. We hold such similar situations that it's uncanny how alike we are and our feelings toward the one person we lost. I decide to open an attachment from Kane. A song of course, Tennessee Whiskey. I listen to the entire song. So relaxing, I close my eyes and listen again and again. I see Shane in this song, he and I dancing slow. My head resting on his chest while his chin placed softly on top of my head. We hold each other tight, swaying back and forth. A lost tear rolls down my cheek, I know to turn off the music and read his caption. I sit back up, wipe the lonely tear away and read his message.

Mistress Miranda,

i am truly blessed You have decided to stay with me. This song i attached reminds me of her. She's smooth, sweet, warm, fuck she is everything i never knew i've wanted or needed. But she is my one and i need her back. i am in a dark place, but i believe the darkness she will love, and she will see good in me. Actually, she has seen my dark and my light. But why didn't she want me? Why did she leave me? i fell Mistress i fell hard but i too am very blessed she entered my life even if i never have her reenter. i had that feeling, that feeling of together. Finally fitting the missing piece that i didn't know existed. This is so hard, i need her Mistress. i need to hold her in my arms. i wish i would have spoken my words before she left. i believe it may not have changed the way she felt but my worries of 'what if' perhaps would disappear. Fuck, Mistress. i am lost, drowning once more and yet writing this all to you helps. i guess i need to hit rock bottom before looking up. This is hell.

Forever,
Kane

I think I read his message ten times. He is absolutely correct about hitting rock bottom. Damn. I am taking advise from my sub. *Why am I doing this Miranda?* Being a Mistress I have no place for. I read it again.

My dearest Kane,

Your message touched My heart deep. Hitting rock bottom is never easy to do or accept. I am at the stage of trying to come to terms with never being in his arms again. Is this the bottom? Will I fly again? I feel very blessed that I met him. He taught Me a lot about life and who I am. I think about him every day almost every second. Your songs hit home, they express My true feelings for him. Memories are a blessing, holding on to them as hope is something you and I need to let go. Unless you are willing and ready to make contact with her. Your 'what if's' need to be answered or you will never heal. Those things that hang will eat us up if we never find answers for them. You need to call her. In fact, I am making that as an assignment for you. I am not pushing, first write down what you wish to say. Go over it a bunch of times until you feel comfortable to call. Then report back to Me. Good Luck.

Always,
Miranda

I pause before I open another, Kane has left yet another attachment and message. This song is I don't wanna live Forever. I can't. I just can't do it. Kane brings up so many memories of Master and I. I want to wash those memories away.

> *Mistress,*
>
> *i hope this finds you well. i am a bit under the weather. Please don't give up on me too.*
>
> *Forever,*
> *Kane*

Since I replied to his first email I leave this one alone. I need to see what my baby Brayden is up too.

> *Mistress Miranda,*
>
> *i couldn't be more correct when i say You have been on my mind every second of the day. i can only imagine what it is my Mistress has in store for me. i love being a good boy for You Mistress, please allow me to continue to further my assistance with You. i will end for now but return shortly only to let You know You are on my mind.*
>
> *Baby boy,*
> *Brayden*

Dearest Brayden,

I have promised you a special gift and I intend to deliver it. I would love to meet in person for this special gift. I will fill in later with more detail for you, until then My sweet boy.

Always,
Mistress Miranda

I opened the last email from Brayden explaining he was thinking of me again. He will be perfect for Sky. She will definitely love him and be a great Alpha female for him. Exactly what he needs. Shutting down the computer I realize a shower is in need. My headache has subsided for the moment and thoughts of Shane pop into mind. He was here this morning helping, worried about last night. I forgot all about it until now, I remember drinking shots with a stranger and then I saw him, Colin. He was there I know it was him for sure. I press harder to my temples. Think Miranda think. I couldn't have imagined-no I didn't. Fuck Colin is in town! Holy shit!

"Sky!" I yell a I grab my towel barley turning off the shower.

"Sky, he was there I remember."

"Who honey?"

"Colin. I was texting you or at least I thought I was but turns out I was texting Shane. Anyways I said 'he's here' and I saw him. I know I did. He was hiding in the back. He had a hat on, grown a beard but I saw him."

"Okay, calm down. I figured he'd find you. He was so determined to."

"I am calm, I think you are the one that's about to explo...." Sky flips out before I can finish my sentence.

"Oh my god Miranda! We need to hide! Call Shane, we need is security."

"Stop Sky. I will not call Shane and ask for security. That will only worry him."

"What are we going to do?"

"There is only one thing to do, is keep living. We just need to be careful, keep our eyes open. If anything looks out of ordinary then you know something isn't right. If you notice an odd person in the crowd watch them."

"Watch them? Miranda that's crazy. Why not get help?"

"Because I want to play his game. I know how he works Sky. Listen, he is watching our every move, so just be careful. He is after me Sky, not you. But you need to keep your head up too, just in case he uses you for bait."

"Oh my god! I'm his bait? I don't want to be his bait," Sky is freaking out, pacing the floor.

"It will be ok, Sky. Trust me. Now let's eat I am starving." I walk into the kitchen, start preparing for but nothing looks good except the frozen peperoni pizza in the freezer. I think to myself that's easy to make and delicious to eat. Pizza it is.

"Sky I'm just going to throw this pizza in the oven. You good with that?"

We eat our pizza in silence. Knowing that we have the same thought scattering around in our brain. One word. One ugly, evil word. Colin.

CHAPTER 8

It's Monday and Colin is still the only thing I can think of. I need to refocus; the fashion show is this Saturday, and much is needed to be finished. Simon is already here and working hard to complete his portion of this project. I don't know where I'd be without him.

"Good morning my favorite seamstress," I say planting a kiss on his cheek.

"Good morning sweetheart. By the way, I am your only seamstress, so your comment doesn't apply," He alerts me. I kiss him on the cheek again, I love this man.

"How was your weekend? Are you feeling better?" knowing last week I sent him home due to his family having the stomach flu in the house. "Did everyone catch the flu?"

"Thank you for asking but my house is just fine. The wife was the only one with the stomach bug, so I am guessing it was something she ate or just a bug only she had. I was feeling a bit chilled with cold sweats, but it passed, and I am ready to work. How was your weekend sweetheart? Meet anyone special?" I immediately started to shed tears after he asked.

"Oh, honey I meant nothing by that. Come, sit, tell me darling, what happened?"

Sniffling through my words I told him of my weekend. Starting with my horrible morning with Shane to the stalker, then my night at the club to Shane being in my apartment the next morning worried about me that Colin being here in MN, so we think.

"Honey, that was some weekend you had. I can work if you need time to walk off your overwhelming weekend."

"Thank you but what I need to do is jump back in here and focus. I can't let Shane, Colin, or my horrific weekend get in the way. Let's work."

"Ok honey. Let's work, however, it seems like you got a whole lot done on Friday. I am proud of you honey."

I smile, I am happy with myself I did get a lot done before I left on Friday. We stay focused the remainder of the day and he does not bring up Shane or my weekend but when we do go out for lunch Colin is brought into the factor.

"Miranda, what do you know so far about Colin? Do you know he is here for sure?" He places gently a hand on mine concerned. "I don't mean to worry you, but I would like to know a little more about him, if you have any information to give."

"I know Simon and I appreciate your concerns for me. All I know is he has been released from jail and is after me since he knows where I am now. Back in IL he hurt a lot of people looking for me, got into bar fights, even upset my mother with a ton of questions of my where a bouts. He has a temper, but I wouldn't say he is dangerous. I pissed him off, I ruined his career, so he is ready for revenge." The waiter comes over, good a distraction at least for a minute. We order, and my distraction is gone.

"Are you scared he may harm you, Miranda?"

I shrug my shoulders, "a little a suppose. He may just want to talk things through and it could end up being a wonderful farewell to a miserable time spent dealing with such pressure. I honestly don't know what he has up his sleeve, he has lashed out and threatened many, so maybe it could turn ugly," I look around hoping that is not the case. "I just want it all to be over, everything." What Simon didn't know about my "everything" was that I meant this fall show, my mistress website, my stalker, and whatever you call Shane and I have going on. I want it figured out. I food arrives and just in time because Simon was ready to open his mouth and continue with the topic. We ate in silence but inside my head sure was business. I couldn't stop thinking about Kane and Mr. Michaels. I kept going back and forth between the two until the silence was broken.

"Shall we walk back and finish the line. I can have the models come in tomorrow and do a walk through with you, would you like me to make that call?"

"Yes, please Simon, I love that idea. Thank you so much for everything Simon you have been just the best supporter and help anyone could ever ask for. Please let me buy lunch that's the least I can do."

"I would never allow a lady to spoil in such a way, I will pay for lunch. I enjoy working for you and with you Miranda there is no paying me back for that. Come on let's go finish."

We head back to the studio and I thank my lucky stars that I did not see my trench coat stalker. I chuckle to the name I have given him; trench coat stalker seems properly suited. Simon and I get straight to work making last minute changes which I stress a bit on due to lack of time we have. All in all, another great day.

Simon dropped me off at home, he didn't want me walking alone in the dark. Now it is time to deal with Sky and her million questions on Colin and Shane.

Not even two feet in the door and I hear, "Miranda, come here please."

"Can I take my shoes off first or do you like them on?" Me being a smart ass.

"Funny sweetheart, just get in here please," I find her sitting on the end of her bed and on the floor are scattered articles of Colin and also photos of Shane. She looks up at me, "so, what I have here are the descriptions of Colin's behavior. He is dangerous, he has told me and you personally that he will kill you once he finds you. Now, look over here," she points to the pictures of Shane. "Here we have a gorgeous babe but that's not the focus what I am getting at is the men in black around him. He has protection Miranda, and that is what you need, or I will be burying your sorry ass. You need to tell Shane."

"Are you crazy? Have you lost your mind? I will not ask Shane or anyone for protection. I am fine Sky, it'll be okay." I start to turn back towards the front door to place my shoes there when I hear, "Well don't say I didn't warn you." I roll my eyes although she can't see it she stills speaks, "I saw that young lady." Returning back into her room, "What did you see?"

"I saw you roll your eyes." I laugh freakishly loud.

"I totally did too. How did you know?"

"I know you better than I know myself that's how." I turn heading to my room, I had an exhausting day and I would love to see if my sweet boys have left me a message, especially Kane. Nothing. Not a one from any of them. I go back into my last messages and they were the last to respond so it's my turn now. I start with Victor.

> *Victor,*
>
> *I trust this message will find you well. To answer your question, no, I will not be your mistress in real life. This site is for training purposes only, I made sure at the beginning of this process everyone knew this. If there is an attraction or emotional feelings taking a play in this then we need to take a step back and re-evaluate our situation. I just train then I send you out to the real world, I will help introduce some Mistresses to you see if you connect with any of them. Otherwise, you are on your own. I still have so much to show you, so let's continue working unless there is an issue of feelings developing, is there?*
>
> *Mistress Miranda*

Next is Kane.

> *Dear sweet Kane,*
>
> *I am sorry to read that you are under the weather, I hope you feel better soon. I will not instruct anything from you until your health is better. If I were in your presence I would*

tend to you as in bringing you warm liquids, laying with you knowing you are loved and cared for. I would play soft music, run baths for you. As I would assume if things were turned you would reciprocate that same love in return. Listen to this song as you rest your eyes. It is a soothing piano calmness, let your mind go, let your body be limp, and rest. I will be checking in but please don't feel obligated to respond only when you feel well again.

Always,
Mistress Miranda

Now Brayden, this is exhausting.

Brayden boy,

Please do not excite yourself too much with the gift I wish to present you with. This is a very special and you have earned it, however it takes time so with that in mind I will suggest another task for you but for now enjoy your evening, I will be returning.

Mistress Miranda

I turn off the computer and play the same piano tune I sent to Kane. I need to relax, this week is going to be stressful, exciting, demanding, nerve racking, it's going to be an emotional roller coaster that sums it up. I let my mind relax to the music, but it decides to drift to other distractions, such as; Shane, my baby boys, Colin, the trench coat stalker, my fashion line. Getting frustrated I through my pillow across the room, "I'm never going to fall asleep with my head going crazy!" I say out loud in my room, apparently, I forgot I have a roommate that barges in to my room.

"You alright sweetheart or should I call reinforcement?" she says with a wink. I know where she is going with that.

"No, I don't need Shane over here, I am fine. I just have a lot going on and my brain will not relax and sleep. Shane is on my mind, the fashion line is, Colin and other stuff but I'm tired Sky, I just want to sleep, please help me sleep." She picks up the pillow I through across the room, "move over," she says and lays next to me.

"I'll lay with you until your pretty little brain falls asleep. Go on, close your eyes." I do as she says, and I feel her hand gently massaging my head, this feels nice, real nice. I fall asleep.

When I wake, it's early yet and I have time to reflect on my morning, no rushing about it. I make coffee, take a long shower, slowly get ready, and then enjoy my coffee outside on the balcony watching the morning dew lift and the sun rise. I need to do this more often, this is happiness, this is heaven. My mind does not think of anything but only enjoys the beauty of this morning, in which I hope to enjoy more mornings like this. I finish my coffee head to gather my papers and work items, I'll disappear today and focus godly on my work only. I can do this, I was born for this challenge. I'm off.

As I walk to my work building, I continue to take in the crisp air, the glare of the sun shining off glass or the wet due making nature appear more presentable. That's it, that is what I need to do just make my line more presentable, more eccentric then the rest and it's simple all I need to do is add one extra flare to each item and BAM! I have created a fall line, one to knock the audience off their seats. I beat everyone into the building this morning and I am thankful for this. I begin immediately drawing out my new ideas to make my line sparkle, stand out, woo the crowd. By the time Simon and a few of the other workers arrive I am on my last design.

"Good morning sunshine, I see you are squaring away deep into work. May I ask what you have there?"

"Sunshine is the [perfect word used for this, that's where I got my inspiration. I woke this morning to see the world for once without distraction. I watched as the sun glistened its rays upon this earth. I saw that just the slightest effort created more and that's when I realized I need one small detail to add to each outfit. Make it shine." I hand them the designs I drew up, "so what do you think? We have time to add this right?"

"This is marvelous Miranda," Simon speaks first, "yes, we have plenty of time to add these designs in."

"This is perfect Miss Miranda." A co-worker says.

"Thank you, both, truly. I am so excited for this!" I show it by my expression jumping and hugging everyone. "Okay, let's get to work." We work through breakfast and late into lunch when finally, I listen to my stomach. "I need food, anyone else want food?" I let everyone leave for an hour and a half, go stretch their legs, get some fresh air. I leave and make my way to Struddles, a café nearby, I order a sandwich to go and walk down to the park. Peaceful. I watch children run around, mothers having conversations with each other, ducks flying in and out of the pond. I enjoy life while I sit there eating my food, pleased with the work we managed to get done. I have the best team ever, I think to myself I will definitely need to buy a gift for all their hard work and my rude behavior. I try to think of ideas when I see him, Shane. I watch as he escorts a beautiful lady into a car and then he slides in next to her. He didn't notice me and why would he, however, my heart did explode seeing him and with another female. He didn't look happy though, he seemed tired, stressed but what would I know plus he was a good distance away. I continue to watch the children, but my mind shifts to Shane. I can't take it any more I get up and head back to the office.

The day continues to cruise like no other and we are finished with the added designs to the fall line outfits. I couldn't be more pleased nor excited to see if this will go the way I am hoping. You will either love it or hate it, I'm praying on everyone to love it. Tonight, I suggest I walk home and tell Simon I will be just fine, I need to walk off the busy day we had tomorrow is going to be just as bad and hard. He doesn't like it but allows it. As I turn the corner to my apartment studio I see my trench coat stalker but this time they are focused on a car down the street and not me. I hide behind the corner and watch curiously. Who is in that car and why does it hold the stalkers attention. I don't anyone get in or out of the car, it's a fancy town car one that Mr. Michaels would have to drive him around. I watched for about five minutes which seemed like an hour, still the stalker continued to watch the car, so I slowly snuck around the building and quickly let myself in the door. Once in my apartment I quickly went to the side window to get a view but no such luck. My window doesn't face that side of the road, sadly. I hear Sky in the shower at this late of the night, I wonder what plans she has for tonight. I sit on the couch and wait to question her.

I hear the bathroom door open and immediately corner her.

"A shower this time of the evening? What are your plans, I am curious to know?"

"Well, Miss nosey, I was thinking of taking you out to dinner you have been working so hard these past days, plus I had an interview with a discussing scum bag that I had to cleanse myself from his odor. You up for going out, I promise dinner only maybe a drink, but I will call it an early night."

"I'd love that, thank you for thinking of me. An interview? I didn't know you had started looking for a job."

"This was last minute, and I was shocked I got called just as quick. I thought we could do oriental cuisine tonight. I found this delicious place past Fourth Street, I guess I don't know if it is good at all but smelt heavenly. Since then I have been craving it."

"That does sound great! I'm game to try it. Have you applied to many places for a job?"

"No just two, this scum bag was one of the two and I just applied so it was crazy and kind of a red flag that he had called so quick in return. I'm not going to back to that place, I refuse to work for a man that hires attractive women and thinks flirting with them is ok."

"Ick that is horrible Sky, I am sorry you had to experience that. If you need a job I could use a bookie," I wink at her knowing she loves to gamble and is great with numbers.

"Me and you work together you know that spells disaster, right?" We laugh as we exit the apartment.

The food was excellent mixed with wine, I am now officially stuffed and tired.

"Thank you for tonight Sky. I am so glad and grateful you are here. Good night." I head down the hall as she enters her room just as stuffed as I am, "good night honey." I know I crashed hard and was sound to sleep, I'm guessing she did the same.

One day left until Show time. Today was actually an easy day. I delivered the designs to the hotel the show is being held at, got the names on each outfit for models to know which theirs is to wear. I sent most of my team home early, Simon stayed back which I knew he would. We went over everything about ten times making sure we it all correct. Now that I was ready all that is left for me is to get a good night's sleep and be at the hotel extremely early in the morning.

CHAPTER 9

It's fashion show time!! I peek out from behind the curtain. The place is starting to get packed. I see my friends Jake, he brought Kyle. Sky is sitting next to Jake. They all look fabulous wearing items I designed. However, backstage is a mess. Unorganized, models everywhere, make-up artist, designers all running around it's a mad chaos. Here, I am, looking out in the crowd and I spot him, Mr. Michaels. What the fuck is he doing here? He has a lady on each arm, one his sister, Faith and the other is Lady Nikki. My heart went straight to my stomach. I feel sick now. Just at that moment I am tapped on the shoulder, Simon.

"Hey cupcake you just see a ghost? Are you feeling alright, Miranda? I got this if you need to get some fresh air, I was just going to tell you your models are ready," He pulls me in for a hug. "Are you ready Miranda?" I nod as I force a smile. Luckily backstage kept me busy and focused so I didn't think of him until it was time to take my seat.

I have five minutes before the show starts. All my models look fabulous. I couldn't be prouder of my team and myself. Crossing my fingers, I land a deal with a major department line. I find my place between Jake and Sky. As I look up across the stage there he sits. Mr. Shane Michaels.

Lady Nikki couldn't be any closer and Faith, his sister is anxiously waiting for the show to start. My stare continues to watch him even when the host announces the designers, my eyes are glued to him. He too is completely stuck on my appearance. I am wearing the dress he so graciously gifted me with. I tried my hardest to pull away from his captive hold, I managed once, when my line came out. I watched as the crowd took in every design of mine that came out on the models. People scooting forward on their seats to inch in at a better look. I heard whispers, I saw smiles, and nods of approval. My stomach started to do flips, I pressed a smile upon my own face. That is when I looked back at him. His glare still holding its place on me, I wonder if it ever left. He bowed his head and winked. That's when I couldn't breathe anymore, and I had to leave. I started feeling nausea. I wanted to cry. I looked at Sky and left my seat.

I remained in the restroom until I knew it was safe to come out. That was a mistake. Shane was standing in the hallway waiting for me. I gave him a quick look before trying to hustle away.

"Miranda, wait. Are you feeling well?" I turn and now we are standing face to face. Again, I have that feeling of wanting to vomit all over my feet or cry because the man I love is here supporting me but he doesn't love me back. I look up directly into his gorgeous eyes, my heart tears. Look away.

"Master, Shane, Michaels, I mean…." My eyes searching for another target, a distraction so I can breathe again.

"Miranda, let me get you some water," he starts going for the fountain next to a waiter. I stop him in mid glide.

"Mr. Michaels, thank you but no thank you. I need to get back in there. I'm feeling better."

"Please let me walk with you," he places his hand under my elbow as we walk side by side, it's dreadful. A beautiful nightmare. Entering the ballroom, I nod to him for my thank you for escorting me back. I disconnect our hold but he pulls me into him. "You look absolutely stunning Miranda," I smile and walk the opposite way of him to my seat. I noticed he stood and watched me until I sat, then he went back to his chair. The models continued to strut their beauty down the run way and people are taking notes, nodding their heads. I watch as my line is next. My face lights up, I am so proud. I hear lots of chattering going on by many spectators. I also see pleased faces from major department stores. Some of the major stores I would love to see my line in, is, Bradstrums, Rose n Main, and Lucky choo. I mean I'd be ecstatic if any one liked my line in their stores.

The show has ended and now it is time to meet the designers. All five of us are called up to the stage. Only one though will receive the achievement of honor. So that means one of the big department stores will own your line but also market it other department stores. Standing on stage I can feel heat bore into my skin and this is not from Mr. Michaels, it is from Lady Nikki. She is glaring, piercing me with those eyes. She holds a smug smile across her face as she reaches for Shane's hand. I look at him and he is holding a huge smile. Pleased with me and I can feel how proud he is of me. It sparks something fierce inside, so I return my gaze back to Lady Nikki and smile at her. Her expression was priceless as her face dropped to a blank pause, knowing I have him. He is mine. Finally, I feel powerful. I can conquer the world and then I hear my name being called and loud cheers. Oh shit! What just happened? I was being too proud, making my stand with Lady Nikki. I am handed the achievement of designer's award proudly presented by Becky Rose and Terri Main themselves. I am trying to hide my over excited expressions but I jump up and down, hug and squeeze them. I couldn't stop saying thank you. They're probably regretting my line now. Thinking she's a crazy one, let's rethink this.

After the ballroom has cleared out, backstage is cleaned up and I have thanked my models. I begin to exit. I open the door the hallway and the people have continued to congregate around. Then I am swamped by the press.

"there she is guys," as a huge crowd rushes over to me.

"Miranda, Miranda," my name is coming from all different direction. I pick the first one up front.

"yes," I say nodding at the lady in front.

"Miranda are you excited to be the next new addition to Rose n Main?"

"Of course, I can't even get a grasp on the correct words to express my excitement. I knew I had a beautiful, creative line, but so did the other designers. I bet this was a tough decision that the judges had," I turn to see Shane making his way towards me and Faith jumping in front of him yelling my name. She is so sweet, I truly enjoy her. My eyes however are clued to another. A man walking behind her, a man with power, a man with desire, a man I fell in love with and a man I continue to love. I have more reporters calling out my name and asking questions, just as Shane steps up behind me. I freeze just for a moment until I see a flash. Someone just took a picture of Shane and I next to each other. He places a hand on my lower backside and I can feel the heat radiating from my inner loins just by this simple gesture. My body goes completely frozen. I turn to an older man, still with Shane next to me and still with his hand on me.

"yes sir," I say to the older gentleman with a polite smile.

"Is this your husband?" Shocked at the question, I turn to look up at Shane and I smile, he returns one back. Hypnotized in a trance of gorgeous eyes peering back at me, we stay connected for only a moment length when a flash tears us a part.

"Miss, my question," the man remarks again.

"No this is not my husband. He is a dear friend of mine," I look back up to see disappointment but approval in Shane's face. That look makes me question his thoughts. I turn back to the reporters, "any more questions?" A few raise their hands and I point to a woman wearing a red scarf around her head. She has light blue eye shadow on that reaches her eyebrow which are penciled in. Her cheeks a rose pink to match her lip stick. I find this woman intriguing only because she has no sense of style but yet at a fashion show.

"What's your next line going to be?" She asks. I try hard not to look confused or distressed only due to that I just was offered a contract with the line that was displayed here on the runway. So, I guess by the looks of it, everyone surrounding her question is in the works of confusion right now.

I chuckle a bit before responding, "I assume I will create a new line eventually. However, I will be busy making the line that had presented itself here today," I hope she understands this answer. Now she is the one with confusion wrapped across her face. Shane bends down and whispers into My ear. His warm breath causes me to close my eyes, as I inhale his scent, I can feel myself lean into him. Then he is pulled away from me. Lady Nikki has drawn his attention. It hurts I will admit, this is my moment he wanted to spend it with me, he came to me and she pulls him away. I know everyone can see my expression drop, my eyes swollen ready to release water drops. I make my way through the crowd, down the hall and into the restroom where I already once was this evening. Sky has followed me in there.

"Hey sweetie you ok? I saw what just happened," I stay silent. "Hey Miranda?"

"What?" I manage to snarl out.

"You can answer the first time you know."

"Do you think everyone else noticed too?" I am terrified of her answer, but I know what it'll be. She lets out her honesty by telling me, "Yes, they saw and they talked and took pictures. Mr. Michaels followed me too. I'm guessing he is outside waiting for your appearance."

"Tell him to go away," I sniffle the words out.

"You know he is a man that stands his ground right, he does what he wants and listens to no one specially if that someone is you he is worried about. I am afraid I cannot stop him. You are going to get cleaned up. Pat the blotches on your face, put a smile on and walk the fuck out," she's very demanding, reason she'll be a great fit for Brayden. I open the stall of the actually very clean restroom. Slowly drag my feet to the mirror. I don't want to look up. I do.

"Ahhhh! What the fuck! How could I look this bad? I don't even wear that much makeup." Now more nervous than ever to leave the restroom, I know that the reporters followed him as well.

"Sky! I can't go out there. Will you please see who is exactly waiting," I clean up my mascara, Sky makes her way out the door. I hear her speaking to someone and then the door is opening again. Still cleaning my destroyed face, I ask, "So how bad is it?"

"How bad is what?" A deep voice that I happen to know so well and adore echoes the restroom.

"Shane," I say startled, turning towards him, "you can't be in here."

"It's never stopped us before," flashing his smirk. He walks further in the restroom, stops inches from me. He wipes the smeared mascara from one eye. "You could never look bad, Precious."

Blushing I can't look anywhere but down. I want to kiss him. I want to hug him. I want to tell him I love him. My heart begins to ache, he stretches his arms out and buries my body into him. As I stay still wrapped in his arms, taking every breath in smelling his scent, feeling his warmth, claiming his hold he has on me. "I want to say I am so proud of you Precious," still holding me he continues to speak. "I always knew you had it in you to be a brilliant, strong, fierce women. Your talent comes so natural to you, gifting other females your fashion so they can feel as powerful as you are." Tears begin to fall slowly however, I control them before he takes notice. "I wanted to say these words in private, just not this way, in a restroom with tons of reporters just outside." I look up, "tons? Did you say tons of reporters?"

"Precious no need to worry, your friend is taking care of them all. She's a good friend to have, extremely pushy too," he smiles down at me and again I melt. "I must return to my company Precious. I hope we can find time and have coffee or dinner soon. I miss you Precious, too much I fear." I squeeze him tight as more tears escape and he kisses the top of my head, releases me from his wrapped arms and exits the restroom. I stay in a bit longer, seems like hours but it's only minutes until Sky comes in.

"Are you alright honey?" Placing a comforting hand on my shoulder.

"Yeah, I am. I'll be out in a minute. Are there still reporters outside?" I ask, which would cause my restroom stay a bit longer.

"No honey I got rid of them for you," she kisses my temple before saying, "see you back at home?" I nod, yes. I give it another few minutes before I leave. I keep my head down as I walk the hallways and enter the parking ramp. Looking for my car I see the trench coat stalker standing remarkably close to my vehicle. I pause and panic. Searching for my phone in case I need it, but when I look up they are gone. Panic really starts to set in, looking all around for my next encounter to appear. I make a fast dash to my car, swing the door open, slam it shut and lock all doors. I'm peeling out of there like I am on the Fast n Furious movie. I continue to watch my review mirror as I drive home, nothing suspicious or out of normal happened. I was safe.

Still with my heart racing, I run up to my apartment out of breath. The slamming the door I turn around and see everyone gathered waiting to scream cheers, but instead drop their excited looks, now they give me the look of questioning.

"Miranda, what is this all about? You look like you've seen a ghost," Jake ask concerned. I guess I did just see a ghost, a ghost that has been haunting me since I've been here on my own.

"I am fine guys, just still shocked by the show today. I mean that was awesome right!" I calming walk more into the apartment with a sly smile hoping to fool everyone. "I mean how cool is it that I won, right? Let's celebrate guys," I don't think they are buying my act, maybe Kyle, but that's because he doesn't know me that well.

"You can't fool me Miranda. What the hell happened from the restroom at the Hall to here?" She is good, giving me her stare down, which works, my body does have the chills.

"It's a long story, we are going to want to sit down for this," as we all gather from the kitchen into the more comfortable furniture. I stand in the middle of the room, spot light on me. I work better if I stand, my brain receives more oxygen this way.

"So, you all know I started working for Mr. Michaels as his maid. He and I began talking…. a lot. He is into BDSM. Do you all know or heard of this, yes?" They all nod, good I didn't want to explain. I continue, "I was curious myself so one night he and I discussed roles. I am an independent woman wanting her freedom so he, being Mr. Michaels said he would train me as a Mistress Domme. He would role switch, meaning he would be my sub and at other times he would be my Master. I began to develop feelings for Mr. Michaels, deep feelings. I love him actually. I'm sure you all knew this. But that failed. He does not love nor have relationships. He had subs that did come into the house, one in particular. Lady Nikki. She is now training to be a Mistress as well. I know she and Mr. Michaels go way back but I don't know the depth of their relationship. It did and does bother me. It also is not my place to worry because he wants nothing to do with me. So, I left him when I knew my feelings were too strong and when Colin got out of jail and came looking for me here," I stop to get a drink mouth is getting a bit dry.

I continue…

"Once I came here and started my fashion business, I also started a website. Mistress Miranda did. I have three subs I am working with, it's rather fun. However, since I have left Mr. Michaels house I have a follower. I notice this person whom I have decided to give them the name of 'trench coat stalker'. It could be male or female but I am assuming it's a male. This person is tall and lean or thin. Always wearing the trench coat and a top hat. A black trilby style hat. I haven't seen them up close, so I have no idea if facial hair exists or not. They are at a far distance and seems to remain that way. At times I believe they are more afraid of me than I am of them. At first, I thought it was Mr. Michaels watching me. But the day I met him at the café shop I saw my trench coat stalker. That changed my mind about him being my stalker. Now I think it maybe Colin but the physique doesn't fit. Colin is shorter and broad shoulders, it doesn't match up. Tonight, after the show, I walked to my car and the trench coat stalker was there, in the parking ramp a little too close this time. Reason I was out of breath when I returned here. My heart still hasn't calmed itself. The night also at the club, I thought I saw

Colin there in a baseball cap. He has to be in town here, don't you all think?"

"Jesus Miranda, you've been going through all of this and not once did you tell us. I don't know whether to smack you or hug you," Jake says coming at me, embracing me in his arms. I hold tight. I miss the hug of a strong man. I notice Skylar is pacing. I watch her as I am still wrapped in Jakes hold. I think she may blow, her mind is working wonders, her hands are flopping all over, and her lips are moving but no sound is coming out yet. She stops, she glares at me, I grab Jake tighter.

"Miranda Scott! I am disappointed in you!" she yells while coming at me. "Do you have any idea how stupid you are for not telling us the danger you could be in? This seriously could be Colin. He said he'd find you and he has been trying and trying real hard. With you out in public all over social media and the newspaper, he's bound to have found you and spy on you," she turns away still flopping her arms in the air. Oh, she's coming back. "Also, Mr. Michaels is in love with you too. You both are just too ignorant to notice!" That statement made me wince. Is he? Could he be in love with me? Still holding tight to Jake my mind is lost on theory that Mr. Michaels may have feelings that run deeper than average for me.

I rest my chin on Jakes chest looking at his adams apple. "Do you think Mr. Michaels could be in love with me?" I ask him. Cupping the both sides of my face into his hands, he looks down at me. "He'd be a fool not too," he places a soft kiss to my lips. A friendship kiss.

After my story, we all took some time to sit in peace and quiet. I reflected on my day, which made me spring off the couch. "Holy shit guys! I got the award for my line with Rose n Main." My surprise of excitement startled them all. "We need to celebrate!" I say as they all agree.

"I'll call Mr. Michaels," I turn in shock as Sky smiles back at me.

"No, I don't believe we need to do that. He is fine doing whatever he has planned tonight."

"Do you really think so Miranda? I bet he is thinking of you right now wondering if you are out celebrating the one thing he is so proud of you for doing. I mean Christ girl, he bought you a dress for the occasion. If that doesn't scream he is into you and thinks about you all the time then I will say you are nuts!"

"I'm sorry but I am going to have to agree with Sky on this Miranda," Jake beautifully adds in.

"Okay guys, I'll let him know where we will be and mention he is welcomed if available." I really did not want to invite him. Today was enough visual of his gorgeous face. I stared at my phone as I had his number pulled up.

"If you don't do it you know I will and that'll be weird because he would rather hear from you. It's sincerer if you invite him."

"I know, I know. I'm doing it so y'all can chill." I say as I walk away for more privacy. Shutting to the door to my room I press send.

"Precious, is everything alright?" That's hi way of saying 'hello' I assume.

"Of course, I just wanted to say thank you again for the kind gratitude you bestowed upon me this evening. It was a pleasure to see you as always. I also wanted to invite you and Faith out tonight if your schedule is free. My friends and I are thinking of celebrating my accomplishments at The Loon on Twin Street downtown Minneapolis."

"I am honored you have thought of us. We would love to celebrate a toast to you and with you for your amazing success." My heart flipped, he can be so dang adorable.

"I look forward to seeing the both of you later. Bye Master." I hung up the phone and realized I had called him Master. This was a mistake. I decide to open my computer to catch up on my sweet boys. It has been a long since I have reached out to them. I've been so busy. I have a ton of messages, close the computer. I realized I can't deal with that right now as well. Rolling over on my bed, decisions on what to wear, as if she read my mind, Sky comes storming in.

"I know exactly what you should wear," entering my closet she goes to the far back. "This," holding up my tiny black dress. "It says I am a goddess. Powerful, beautiful, and smart. Yep, this is what you are wearing tonight," she looks at me waiting for me to protest. "Good we agree then." Setting the dress on my bed she exits the room. I pick up the dress, *how am I going to fit in this?*

Squeezing my best into this dress or so called "dress" I pull it on and stare at myself in the full-length mirror hanging on the back of my bedroom door. Leave the hair down, still looks decent from today's earlier events. Slap on some lip gloss and I am ready. I open the door and strut my most confident walk, "Let's go!" I say. I think to myself let's just get this night over with.

The Loons bar is packed; however, we are directed to a reserved table thanks to Mr. Michaels calling and arriving beforehand and using his powers to receive special attention. He is seated at the end of the table with Faith along his side. They both zoomed in on me. Faith with the biggest smile and Mr. Michaels with a smirk which made his eyes sparkle. My heart melted. He is a sexy god, wearing a white button up dress shirt and of course he had the first few buttons undone, his black trousers fit his ass perfectly along with black belt and a shiny silver buckle. Standing tall and confident pouring out power. Faith stole my stare from him and captured me into a hug. My friends followed behind, greeting themselves around the table. We all ordered drinks and once everyone hand their beverage in their hand it was then he stood on a chair. Yes, Mr. Michaels, Master stood up on a chair to receive the entire bars attention and he did. Every one turned toward the sexy god on the chair waiting for his next move, I however hid behind Sky.

"Attention everyone! May I have your attention! Thank you," He says to the crowd as if he owns everyone in the bar, I feel my cheeks flush. "Tonight, my group here is gathering to celebrate a talent young beautiful Lady and her accomplishments not only has she received a major title today, but I believe this woman can do anything her lovely heart desires. My dear sweet Precious, you have conquered one item on your list, may you have the same results with the rest of your dreams. To Miranda!" Cheers throughout the bar as they all salute my name, "To Miranda!" I silently thank the crowd by raising my drink to them back. I turn immediately to Shane. He stands proud with a smile. Then he does what I love most…he winks. I strut my sexy little black tight dress his way, give him a half smile before I decide my choice of words.

"Thank you for that speech and using your powers to get us a table. Man, this place is crowded," turning my attention back to him. "I mean it, thank you for everything. For my dress, for supporting me this whole time and now this," I gesture my hands around. "I'm really glad you came tonight. I umm I need to say something Master but it's…." I am interrupted by my friends and a tray of shots. As they push their way through I am handed a shot, then another and another. By the time I leave the bar I am carried out. Too many shots, way too many. I pass out as soon as my head hits the pillow…I think it was my pillow.

CHAPTER 10

My eyes slowly, very slowly manage to open. Thank god someone closed my curtains. My eyes focus to the room I am in, oh good it's mine. I have a pounding head ache, I will kill who ever handed me all those shots last night. I remember I was going to connect with my baby boys but closed my computer. Thank the good lords I didn't reach out considering the mess I was last night. I remind myself today I better acknowledge them. Not now though my head is hurting, and the bright screen will cause more excruciating pain. Curiosity eats at my thoughts. I roll back over, stare at the computer. I am anxious to see what my boys have been up too. So, I grab the computer, flip it open and plug away.

Wow! I say to myself there is a lot of messages. I begin with Victor. He has been requesting a meet face to face.

Dearest Mistress

May i be of service to You more? I wish to fulfill every deep fantasy You desire. i feel i am the man to be that particular sub You

> *need at Your side. Tell me, what can i do to*
> *please You?*
>
> *Your man,*
> *Victor*

I get a sense from Victor that he is not ready to be a sub yet. He likes control and I don't see this a roll for him. Perhaps, I should mix or suggest he train as a Dom. I would, however, need to meet in person with him. I believe that way I can read him better, get more of a feel to who he really is. What his intentions are. He is my aggressive one, very eager to rise above the rest. Which can be a little scary as well. A Mistress should not be afraid of her subs.

> *Dearest Victor,*
>
> *I adore your eagerness to fulfill My deep desires. Trust Me darling you are and will continue to please Your Mistress. I wish to hold a meeting soon, very soon with you. In the meantime, please tell Me a dark secret you would like to have played out as a fantasy. There is no time frame I am giving you. Think of this assignment wisely, I'd like to make it worth your while.*
>
> *Mistress Miranda*

My main focus is Kane. As I have stated all along he holds a very dear spot to my heart. I feel his pain, it hits so close to home. The way I feel for Master, just as he does for his lady. I wonder if he has reached out to her as I had suggested he need to do. He needs closure, or I don't see him ever healing. I open his emails and I see only one has an attachment, the last one.

Mistress,

i have been drowning in a dark cloud for some time now. i see her, i see often. i can't stay away. i am drawn to her, she is my addiction, my favorite drug that seeps through my veins. When she was mine she was my cure. i saw her. i waved when she saw me. She waved back but also had an awkward look upon her face as if i shouldn't have been in her part of town. i didn't have the courage to speak to her then hopefully next time i will. i need your help Mistress, You shed light and give me faith. i need the strength to see her face to face. i know You must be busy. i won't do anything next until i hear from You.

Forever,
Kane

Dear lord, I hope he didn't wait. I haven't been exactly the best Mistress lately. I open the next email from him, this one doesn't have the attachment only a paragraph.

Mistress Miranda,

i called her. Then i hung up before she could even answer, in fact it didn't even ring. i need her back. my life is completely empty without her in it. i messed up big when i let her go. i should have a held her longer, pleaded her to stay with me. i need Your help, i am falling apart.

Forever,
Kane

Tears begin to fall from my eyes. I feel completely awful. I have not been there for these guys. All this tells me, I should not be a Mistress. I really shouldn't. I only did this to distract myself from Shane. This, this while website has only has made me think more often of him. I should find myself first before ever taking in subs or training even. I open the last one from Kane along with the attachment. Another song by Zayn and Taylor Swift, I don't want to live forever.

Mistress,

i am in a dark hole today. i thought if maybe i went over in her area i would get closure. Perhaps see her with another, which would have killed me, but i would have known then to move on. However, instead of just spying on her, i decided to walk the streets just as i was turning a corner a young girl ran into me. Her, being the young girl. i caught her before she hit the ground. i rubbed my hand down her cheek. Remembering how smooth her skin is. i looked into her eyes, she was cold, her look that is. i immediately placed her on her feet. My thoughts couldn't escape her look. It was an expression of what the hell are you doing here. She didn't seem a bit excited to see me. Although i was asked to join her inside. Our conversation was short and stiff. i ran off rather too quickly. i was hurting inside. My heart was bleeding once again. Mistress, i told her i missed her. Her response…nothing. Mistress i miss her so much. i miss the taste of her kiss. The small moans she made whether i be pleasing her or her just enjoying a delicious donut. The hum, i miss her hum when she wrapped her soft lips delicately around my cock. The vibration was pure torture-good torture. Her touch was a warmth that held a powerful electric force, a damn good force. Her smile was my comfort place, a place i call home. Mistress she took my breath away. No one has ever loved me, no one has ever tried and then she appeared. i thought my worst was over until she walked away from me. Now i am locked in this nightmare. i want out.

Forever,
Kane

I grab the tissue box off my nightstand. Dab my face, wipe my tears. His story is utterly a mirror of my relationship with Shane. I honestly have no idea how to reply back. I reply all the times I have ran into Mr. Michaels, all our chats, our hidden looks, secretive touches. I know exactly how Kane is feeling. The song, my dear lord it screams pain.

Dear Kane,

I would like to send my deepest apologizes. I have not been here for you but instead taking care of My needs. I wish I could give you professional advice. I wish I could cure your pain. I say this because I know it all too well. When My world is falling apart and there's not a light to break up the dark, that's when I look at him. He is My comfort. He is My calm. I feel as if the ocean waves are flooding the shore and I can't find My way home. He was My home. I have lost My way. I try to keep busy in work and I thought having My own Mistress website in which he helped train me would occupy my distraction of him. It doesn't. I believe you just need to pour your heart out to her. If you don't, you will always wonder what if. Maybe she needed time to figure it out herself. Maybe she will say she's better off. I can't help you there My sweet boy,

but I will say, try. Try to call her, ask to meet.
Lay everything on the table. At least try.

Always,
Mistress Miranda

Satisfied with my response, I begin to think maybe I should take my own advice. Lay everything out on the table with Mr. Michaels. But when? Maybe over the phone, I couldn't bear to see his face when he is denying any affection for me. This is hard. Why did I tell Kane to do it if I can't be that strong myself? I look at the messages from Brayden. I need to set up a meeting time with him and introduce Skylar. Then my next move will be to meet with Victor. Release him to a tough Mistress, he needs an alpha female with power. I can't handle him. Then maybe Kane would like to meet. I can't have this website anymore though. Not until I get my life straighten out. I open Brayden's emails. He is a good boy, such a pleaser. He mentions wanting to do more for me, to act out my every desire I wish for him. My desire is he take care of Sky.

Sweet baby boy,

I want to thank you for your time submitting to Me, your Mistress. I can no longer take on this roll as I need to get My life figured out. I am going to recommend you to a dear friend of Mine. I would like to meet you this Tuesday at Struddles. It's a café near the main strip uptown Minneapolis. I will send further information with this meeting but in

> *the meantime can you explain to Me what the*
> *definition to submitting means to you. I am*
> *extremely excited for you to meet this friend*
> *of Mine. I have a really good feeling you both*
> *will be a perfect fit for each other. After our*
> *meeting I will be shutting down My website.*
> *I have been blessed to work with you. I'm*
> *looking forward to our meeting.*
>
> *Always,*
> *Mistress Miranda*

I close my computer feeling better but not complete. Ok, to be honest, I am miserable after reading all those messages. What would Shane think of me? Leaving my subs like that for a long period of time. All of them seemed hurt in some form or other. I lay a bit longer in bed, staring up at my ceiling. *Should I take my advice and meet with Shane?* No, no I can't. I shut my eyes. I picture the two of us meeting. I see myself expressing my feelings I have towards him. Then, I see him telling me, those were not his intentions. He was merely training me for the world I wanted to enter. Oh. My. Gerd. That's exactly what he will say. I can't meet him. Stressed with a headache, I remain still. Stiff as a board.

"Miranda? You up?" I hear my beautiful friend say through the closed door.

"Unfortunately, yes, I am," I say mumbling into my pillow.

"Good. May I come in then?"

"Yes," still mumbling into my pillow. I lay still, face down, eyes closed.

"Miranda, do you need me to get you anything?" I hear a slight giggle out of her that causes me to turn just a tiny inch.

"Laugh all you want honey. I'm wrecked," now half of my face smashed into the pillow.

"Get up, take a hot shower, have a cup of coffee, and eat something greasy. Then you'll need to take a big dump and you'll feel much better," she says while ripping the sheets off me.

"You think taking a big dump makes it all better?" Flipping my body over now.

"It does me. Makes me feel like I am emptying all the alcohol out of my system."

"Ok. Let's leave that conversation for another day. I do have something I need to talk to you about though. But first, that hot shower," I say as I slowly roll out of bed. Walking down the hall hurts my eyes by the small light that is seeping in through the curtains. I turn on the shower, blast it to hot so it heats up faster, at least that's what I think. Steam starts to hit the mirror and I know it's time to hop in. Turning the temperature knob down so I my skin doesn't melt off. I stand under the flow of water letting it pour over my head and drain down my body. Closing my eyes, I replay the night. I remember how sexy Shane looked, I remember how proud he was of me. His words of stating I can conquer anything brought my way and I shall continue to with the rest of my dreams. He is my dream. I wonder if he knows or if he was trying to send a hidden message to me. My brain is wrapping on his words and my heart is holding on to them.

Now dried and dressed, I leave my hair to air dry and apply minimal eye makeup. It's time to tell Skylar of my plan.

"Hey Sky, you around?"

"Yes, hun, I'm in the kitchen. What do you need?" I peek my face around the corner.

"We need to talk. It's not serious so don't give me that look. No, you are not in trouble nor am I kicking you out."

"Oh, mer gerd Miranda, spit it out! She shake's my shoulders. Laughing, "ok, ok. Let's sit though, I have a lot to say." We both take a seat at the kitchen table, I have my computer to show her of my website and explain Brayden.

I start by saying, "You remember when I spoke about a mistress website, where I have subs? I call them my baby boys, but you remember?"

"Yes, I do recall," she states.

"Good. I have a sub; his name is Brayden. Brayden also works for Mr. Michaels, I met him at a gathering Shane was having. He's very attractive and very well-mannered and loves to love a special lady indeed. I had a sexual encounter with him at Shane's gathering. Shane had gotten me all worked up in the kitchen but left me in a heaping mess, so I touched myself, there in the kitchen. When I opened my eyes Brayden was there watching, but not only watching he was getting himself off too. I enjoyed it just as much as he, but then I felt guilty for that feeling when I knew I was falling for Mr. Michaels. I then told Shane of this encounter I had with one of his colleagues and was punished or rewarded in front of Brayden. I don't know if Brayden still works for Shane or not but what I do know is I think he would be a perfect match for you and I would love to set up a meeting.

I have told him about a lady I would like to introduce him to this Tuesday." I take a breather, she looks lost.

"Sky, you good?"

"Holy shit Miranda, what the fuck?"

"What?" I'm confused.

"What the hell have you been up too? From masturbating in front of people to running a mistress hot line and your own designing company yet matching people up. I mean, really, what the fuck."

"You see, I want to end my mistress website. To be honest, I can't take care of my boys when I am a complete mess myself. Who am I to direct them in a positive life style when I'm living in the dark." I hold a long pause. She's thinking. This is good, she has a descent expression, it's not bad. The pause is too long, now I may start to worry.

"Sky, what do you think? Trust me when I say this is a good man, he will not disappoint. He aims to please and you can boss him around, he'll love it. At least meet him with me, please." She puckers her lips, squints hers eyes, stares few a few seconds at me then she finally speaks.

"Okay, yes, I'll do it. I will meet this so-called sub of yours. I have one question though, If I do like him then does that make me is mistress?"

I chuckle, "no it would not make you his mistress. He loves to please his lady, he will spoil you with any desires, wishes you have. This man fits you, I see a forever between you two."

"Hold on there, missy. No one said anything about forever. I am not a forever type of girl," I let her talk, but I have a smile plastered on my face, I know I am right. This will become a forever. I clap my hands together, "so are you in? Will you meet Brayden?"

"Yes, I will meet him. I'll feel bad if he has his hopes up though, I'm not in this for love you know, I'm not looking."

"Believe me, you will like him, and you will have fun. Just try it out, maybe it will turn into something beautiful and if it doesn't then it doesn't. You part your ways and say goodbye," I tell as I get up, "oh by the way meeting Tuesday at Struddles café at noon. Now that I've wasted most of my Sunday, I'm going to go back to bed, so I can function tomorrow at work."

"Hey Miranda?"

"Yeah."

"You wouldn't happen to have a picture of Brayden, would you?" She shrugs her shoulders.

"Of course, I do honey. Come back to my room and I'll pull one up for you. I even have a video."

"A video? What is he doing in the video? Wait, I don't want to know," she giggles, "you kind of have a busy but interesting life I must say."

"The only thing I know about my life being good, is I had Shane in it and I want Shane back in it. Until then, I don't have much if I don't have him." She pats my back noticing the pain through my eyes. We sit on my bed as I reach for the computer and hit Brayden's profile. I pull up a couple of pictures for her. Turning the computer her way, "feel free to scroll through them if you want. I believe just one is enough to make you drool. Am I correct?" I turn to look as she is fanning herself, mouth open, constant blinking. I giggle, he is a site to see but not as sexy as Mr.

Michaels but then again, no one compares to Mr. Michaels of course this being my perspective.

"Holy shit Miranda! He is a god and he wants to serve me, you're saying?"

"Serve? I don't know if that would be the correct term for him. He is very loving and wants to make his lady happy, so he'll do most anything to do such. But with that comes reward. You would need to reward him in return with something he enjoys, makes him happy. Please don't make his life miserable. I'm not saying you will, but he is special, reason I am handing him over to you. I know you will take excellent care of my baby boy," we both laugh at my last comment.

"I can't wait to meet him. Tuesday better hurry."

"I'm glad you are excited. He is too." Her eyes lit up when I said that. I think she already formed a crush on him. "I'm super exhausted, you want me to send you the pictures of him, so you can ogle all night over them?" She smiles back, and I know that means yes please.

I wake to my alarm on the highest setting volume a tiny alarm clock can have. I slam my fist down nearly breaking the tiny box but hurting my hand more. I don't think I have ever slept so good before, well I have in the arms of Shane. I need to call him and let him know of my feelings, just like what I told Kane to do with his past relationship. I push through my thoughts and gather myself for a Monday work day.

Best part about having a roommate is my coffee is always ready for me in the morning. Taking my thermos of warm French vanilla coffee and all my drawings in my briefcase I head to the office. I have a beautiful tune playing in my head, Sheryl Crow, Soak up the sun. Morning walk is full of warmth from the beauty of the sun shining on every step I take. Then, then it all went cold and dark when I spotted my trench coat stalker. Luckily, I am close to the office building, but the chills that this person isn't a friend and watches my every move from afar. Just before I enter my building, I stop. I hold a gaze with my stalker. This time they remain still too, normally this person turns and leaves. In a stare down battle I decide to take one step toward this person like a coward, they reciprocate. My heart pounds faster, fear rising in my throat. I stand my position, waiting for their next move. They pull their top hat down further and turn away, exiting our stare off. My breathing becomes easy and I feel my heart rate slower, I now can get on with my workday.

"Hi Simon!" I yell as I take the first step into the room.

"Hey good morning gorgeous. How was your weekend?" He gives a smirk with his wicked laugh.

"I have a feeling you know something I don't. Please wipe that shit eaten grin off your face. Tell me was I a total wreck on Saturday?"

He gestures with his hand so-so, "not a total wreck but you were good in the bag, isn't that what you young folk say?"

Laughing, "no, not at all. Who says that? Maybe half in the bag but certainly not 'good in the bag', I use quotes around the words when spoken. "Please, did I make a fool of myself?"

"No darling you were just as you should have been. You had plenty to drink, but I believe you handle your liquor content well. And by well, I mean you were still focused which is good, but you were very focused on one particular person. I don't believe I need to say the name."

Tucking a piece of hair behind my ear to hide my embarrassment I say, "no. no need to say names, I perfectly know who you are referring to." I walk back to my desk, stare at the wall.

Suddenly the day is gone, and I hear Simon shout his departure as I return for him to have a great evening with his family. I gather my belongings and head out myself. For tomorrow is the meeting between Brayden and Skylar which I cannot wait for. I wonder if Brayden will remember me? Locking up the building I had a feeling I was being watched. But after surveying the area for my trench coat stalker I realized it is just all in my head.

Once home and inside safely form the world, I put my feet up, grab a glass of wine and my computer. I send Brayden a message to make sure we are still on for tomorrow.

Good evening sweet Brayden

I hope you have had a wonderful Monday, I am looking forward to meeting with you tomorrow. Are you able to make it at noon? Is the café Struddles, down off Main a good place for you to meet? If it is too far out of the way can meet elsewhere. I'll be anxiously waiting for your response.

Always
Mistress

I leave my computer on and open while I get myself ready for bed. I hear my notification sounds as I am washing my face. I quickly bounce on the bed to see if it's Brayden and yes, it is.

> *Mistress Miranda,*
>
> *You have no idea how excited i am to meet You in person. Of course, i will be there tomorrow at Struddles by noon. i am sad to be leaving You Mistress, but i believe You have placed me with a beautiful suture, so i can fulfill her every desire. i will see You tomorrow My beautiful Mistress.*
>
> *Baby boy,*
> *Brayden*

Yes! I close my computer fist pumping the air I am super excited for tomorrow. It's on, yes!

I turn off the lights as in hopefully I will fall asleep soon. Ugh, I can't. I begin to dream of Mr. Michaels. What life would be like with him, would he ask me to marry him, would he want children? I imagined a life that would be filled with laughter, love, so much love. He would make such a wonderful daddy, I see him now playing with the children, kissing them, protecting them. I smile as I drift further into sleep.

I am disturbed from my slumber to a loud beeping sound. The alarm, I love the alarm especially today. I fly out of bed and run in to Sky's room. Jumping on her bed, kissing her while laying on top of her, "Wake up! Today you get to meet a hottie," I say breathing my morning breath on her.

"Get off me you smelly loaf," she says trying to roll me off her. "Nope, no. Get up, lets pick out what you are going to wear today," still lying on top of her, giving her kisses. Slapping my face away and using her legs to get me off, I finally give in. Standing now in her closet, "hmm what should we wear?" I turn to her.

"I already picked out what I am wearing, it's over there." She points to the chair.

"Already picked it out you say, a little excited, are we?"

"Me? Look at you, jumping on me, going through my closet. Now, can you please get out, I didn't get much sleep last night." She says pointing to the door.

"Sure, but was it because you were thinking of him, dreaming and drooling about Mr. sexy?" I giggle and duck out of her room just in time for her to throw a pillow at me, missing and hitting the door as I close it. Noon cannot get her fast enough I say to myself as I enter the kitchen to make coffee which is already brewing thanks to my roommate for starting the timer for this morning on it. So, I decide to take a quick shower and enjoy my coffee on my walk to work. Maybe today I will get more done than I did yesterday.... or maybe not.

"Is it noon yet?" I keep asking Simon.

"No sugar, why do you keep asking? What is happening at noon today?"

"I am meeting a friend at Struddles and introducing her to another friend." I tell Simon

"So, you are setting two people up is what you are saying?"

I jump up, "Yes! Exactly and I can't wait either. Sorry I know I am being annoying, but this is going to be very exciting. I couldn't be happier for these two to finally meet." I am so giddy I can't sit still.

"Why don't you go for a walk before you met with them, I can see you aren't getting much done here nor can you sit still little miss fidget." He chuckles, and I agree I need to go walk off my energy. I walked towards the park, I wanted to admire nature at its finest. I walked the path that leads down to the water, I watched frogs leap from lily pad to lily pad. I listened to the birds chirp a song and smelled the fresh flowers that had blossomed. I reviewed in my head how the meeting was going to play out, hopefully my expectations of this are met. I am ready. I begin walking my way to the café, smiling the whole way.

I find an open table after placing my order. This part is the worst, the waiting.

I see Brayden walk in and I wave to him. He walks over, big smile on his face. He is looking even better than I remember. Fitted jeans and a black polo t-shirt, his dark hair combed perfectly, and his eyes sparkle under the dark shirt.

"Hi Brayden. How are you?" I ask as I stand to give him a hug. He embraces my hug so well I miss a man's touch.

"It's a pleasure seeing you here. I am well, doing excellent actually. I joined a BDSM training with a mistress, Miranda…." He looks at me for a bit, I'm guessing he didn't see this coming. "Mistress?" he asks.

"yes, sweetheart. I am Mistress Miranda." His smile grew bigger, that eased some of my fear quickly. "I had no idea; didn't even cross my mine it could be you. I thought you and Shane." He covers his mouth then points at mc.

"You left Shane, didn't you? That's' the reason he has become a different person. Miranda, we need to talk." We sit down just as my order arrives and he then decides on a drink.

"Miranda, I don't know what happened between you and Shane. As you know he is a private person and you, well, you made him different, good different. It was before you came he was content, happy but something was missing. You. Then you arrived, and he was a whole new man. Brilliant in his work, I mean he was before but even more so now with you in his life. He saw light, he was breathing easy. He enjoyed us guys around before he would be grumpy and make excuses for not joining us on poker night or not being our fourth for golf. He found himself in you when you came. Now, he doesn't even come into the building. He holds all meeting by phone. He does not attend affairs or banquets anymore. He barely talks to us if we are lucky we can get a mumble out of him. Can I ask? What happened between the two of you?" I shift in my seat, I feel warm tears trickle down my cheeks.

"I love him, but he doesn't love me back. I had to leave it got too painful to stay knowing he'd never share the same feelings I have. I wasn't strong enough to tell him of my feelings either. I figured if I did he would want me gone for sure, so, before he could kick me out I held my dignity and left. I tried starting this website and my new fashion business keeping myself busy, thinking then I would have thoughts of him or miss him. I was wrong, I think of him daily if not all day and I miss him. I need him like the stars need the sky." Tears now streaming steady down my cheeks, Brayden gets up and comes to my side of the table wrapping his arms around me.

"Just tell him, I know he feels the same." Brayden adds placing a kiss on my head. I stay in his arms for a while, I need this. Just as we are pulling apart and my face now appears presentable Skylar walks in. Looking sexy as usual she kept her hair down and her smile wide, she's a knock out. I see Brayden's eyes glimmer with hope that this his new lady. I wave over to her to come in our direction. She has a beautiful smile across her face she looks directly at Brayden. She holds her hand out, "Hi I'm Skylar, it's a pleasure to meet you." Brayden stands, he is gorgeous as we both follow his height. He takes her hand pulls it to his mouth for a soft kiss then says, "the pleasure is all mine, my lady." Sky's face turns beet red, I knew it, I knew they would hit it off. My job here is done. Brayden pulls a chair out for Sky as I stand to make my announcement that I am leaving the two to get acquainted. Brayden hugs me, "don't forget what I said Miranda, he needs you just as much as you need him. Call him, please." I pull back from the hug and look up at Brayden, "I'll think about it. I want too but something is holding me back. Disappointment I suppose."

"There is nothing that will disappoint you if you call and meet him. Trust me, he needs you." I embrace another hug, walk around the table to give Sky a hug as well and whisper in her ear, "enjoy." She hugs me, "Thank you and listen to him, please." I leave the two and as I knock on the door, I turn to look back at them, already Brayden is holding her hand across the table, he has a huge smile as he listens intently to everything coming out of Sky's mouth. I'm happy for the two of them.

CHAPTER 11

As suspected Skylar was gone the entire day until night fall. When she arrived home, I could tell she was very pleased and in heaven with her new man. I felt a warm glide of air and happiness swift over me, maybe a self-congratulation as well. I knew they would be perfect for each other as well as fulfilling each other's desires to please. I however have not fulfilled mine, Shane hasn't left my thoughts, but I have no idea how to mention that I love him and need him. I want him back in my life, he completes everything I stand for and everything I have dreamt of. I feel tears fall, fuck I get so emotional when thinking of him. I lean toward my night stand, grab my computer, first I will write a rough draft of what I shall say to him, then I'll decide if I want to actually send it. Why can't he be the man and talk to me, reach out to me? This all sucks. I begin writing my thoughts to say or address the matter. I'd prefer telling him in person my feeling rather than by email, so I need to plan a meeting. The park is a perfect place, I could grab some coffee to go and muffins, we could sit on the bench say what is needed to be said and if all goes awkward then we would have plenty of distractions. I like this, it does perfect. I pull up my emails and begin my message.

Dearest Mr. Michaels,

I hope this letter finds you well. I enjoyed seeing you and Faith at the fashion show and was so pleased you both were able to join the celebrating of the next chapter in my life. This brings up much thought as my next chapter begins, I was wondering if you would so kindly join me at the park, Applewood Park on the south side? I need a friend to confide in and this friend I wish to do just that is you. I truly hope you can find time as I know you run a busy schedule. If you could let me know if this Thursday works for you.

Always,
Miranda

I re-read it and press send. Short and sweet, leaves him in kind but wondering what I may have to say for my next adventure in life. Within minutes I hear the chime I have a new email. Its him. Shane, I find my stomach twist in knots. Why am I nervous? I open his response.

My sweet Precious,

It is always such a pleasure to hear from you, My heart does flips when you contact Me. I would love nothing more than to meet with you in the Park Thursday morning. I shall bring Us some rolls and coffee. I am extremely delighted you want My advice on your next adventures, to your new beginnings.

Forever,
Master

Its uncanny how much we think alike. I smile just as I read of him bringing rolls and coffee for that was my intentions to bring for us too. While I have my computer open I decide to write to my boys one last time. I told Kane he needed to contact his ex as I just did, I can tell him of my effort, hopefully that will give him courage if he hasn't done so already. Victor, I had asked he report a dark secret he would like to act out. I can't wait to see you these two have been up too. I open Kane's first, he has an attachment with it. I open the attachment first, it's a song by Ed Sheeran, Thinking out Loud. I listen to it, this song is perfect, I can relate to it so much. How is it Kane picks songs that identify the same meaning I have for Shane.

Mistress Miranda,

As You heard from the song, if You haven't listened to please do so before You continue to read. Otherwise, this song i never thought i would have swept someone such as her off her feet. i wonder if she remembers the taste of my love, i gave her every flavor starting with vanilla, but i knew she was a swirl of variety with many sparkles. i could see her smile shine through her eyes even when her lips didn't curve. i found love in the most mysterious way and I continued to lover her more and more every single moment wake or not. i miss so much the kiss she would spring on me, the small moans she made when she enjoyed anything, it could have been my touch, or thick juicy steak. The hum...the hum that she made when her soft lips wrapped delicately around my stiff cock. Fuck, she made my world go around. Her touch was a warmth that held a powerful electric bolt, a damn good shock it gave. Her smile was a comfort place a place i call home. When she appeared i thought the worst was over, perhaps it had just begun. i fell in love. i wish she would have cried out for more, i would have done and gone through lengths to keep her. i wish i was stronger and walked through the storm and told her not to go. i am now locked in a nightmare, i want out. i have been reaching out to her, i have been this whole time, she just hasn't seen me yet.

Forever,
Kane

Damn, he has been reaching out to her and she isn't responding. Is she a stupid bitch? What the fuck? I am a little upset with myself for pushing him and she hasn't been reaching out, responding. My heart breaks. I definitely need to tell him how painfully sorry I am.

Dearest Kane,

I am breaking inside, I feel I have pushed Myself to far wishing for you to only contact her and here you have been all along and she not an answer back. I can no longer say anything nice about her and I wish you well. You know I was all excited to inform you that I have contacted the one I thought I had lost. He however, returned the favor as to meet with Me, so I can discuss the next chapter in my life hoping he will take it with me. I never tried to love, never thought it was for me. If I did feel for another I couldn't recognize if the love was for me or my fame. Then I found him, I wasn't looking, he saw me saw even what I didn't, and he showed me. This was who he was though, a gentleman, one I thought didn't love himself. I fell hard for him realizing I should not have and in order to accept that he would never love me I had to walk away. I never wanted to walk but he just didn't love me back or, so I thought. In my head we had something special, I loved every thought about it too. I can't go on living always thinking of him, it hurts. So, I am taking My own advice and I have decided to meet him, let all my feelings out. He needs to hear them, he is a special man and I believe he can find love if he just trusts it. I would love to continue our friendship, perhaps meet

> *soon once all this is done and said. I will*
> *be closing this account however, I will leave*
> *you with My contact information, so you can*
> *reach Me whenever you need to talk. I would*
> *love to grab drinks sometime and meet the*
> *man behind all this, I feel we are very similar.*
>
> *Always*
> *Miranda*

I go back and read Shane's email again, I feel a sense of warmth. I love the way he makes me feel, it's a home feeling, a complete way of relaxation. He is my soulmate if I have ever thought that possible or were to believe in soulmates. I love him. This I know for sure. Victor, I open his email, he gives me a sour taste in my mouth. He is dangerous, I don't trust him.

> *Mistress Miranda,*
>
> *You have asked that i tell You of a dark secret.*
> *My dark secret is revenge. My last lady ran*
> *off on me, i'd like to punish her. i would*
> *enjoy nothing more than to turn the tables*
> *and punish her just as she did me. i want*
> *control and i her to know i have control. No*
> *more running no more lies but to do as i say.*
> *i want her to be my pet. i am sorry to hear*
> *of You leaving, i hope i get a chance to meet*

with You and thank You in person for Your
generous time given.

Your man,
Victor

I had the goose bumps while I read that. He would punish any lady in his hands if given the opportunity. He scares me, I don't know if I could meet him, really, I have no desire too, but I know deep down I should. I owe it to all of my boys.

Dear Victor,

I have always sensed a more dom figure in you
or a possible switch roll manner as well. I hope
your lady comes back to you so you two can
play out your desires. I am sorry as well that I
am leaving but I need to figure so much of my
life out before I can continue to help out with
others and their struggles or better yet needs. I
feel I owe you a meeting and would love to if
this Thursday evening works. I can arrange a
table at the LookOut say around 7ish? I hope
you find your happiness Victor.

Mistress Miranda

I read Shane's email again to get my warm feeling and the creepiness of Victor out of me. I head out to the kitchen thinking a glass of wine and chill on the deck is a nice way to unwind in the quiet dark night. I write everything I want to say in my head for when I see Shane. The night is getting late and I have killed the bottle of wine. I walk back into my room grab my computer, I know this is not a good idea but I'm a little excited and a little buzzed from the wine, so I decide I will write an email to whomever pops up first. Shit, it's Victor. "Ick" I say out loud, I open his email sense he has sent one to me.

> *Mistress Miranda*
>
> *i was very shocked yet relieved You too want to meet for our parting ways. Thursday at the LookOut is a great place. i look forward to our meeting. Have a good evening.*
>
> *Your man*
> *Victor*

This might be a big mistake by meeting him but like I have said, I feel bad dumping these men like I am because I can't figure out my own shit. Blast it all to hell! I look at Kane's email address, I begin to wonder if he is at all able to move on. I wish that bitch of an ex would just reply to him, even if she says leave me alone. That would be something and perhaps all he needs. I notice I have another new email, hoping it's from Shane it is not. Kane has written me another email.

> *My dearest Miranda,*
>
> *i cannot find the words to express how genuinely happy i am for You. i wish nothing*

but the best in Your future endeavors. i am
pleased that this man, this very lucky man has
made the correct decision to meet with You.
i would love nothing more than to introduce
myself to the brilliant Miss Miranda. May we
as well meet? i have Thursday open.

Forever yours,
Kane

He uses words just as Mr. Michaels does, I love how he speaks. Thursday? My Thursday is booked, although it would be smart to meet with him at the same time I meet Victor, this way I am not alone with him. I am being cautious, Victor scares me, a little too much. The week is dragging, I knew this would happen because I am so excited yet nauseas about meeting Shane. Victor and Kane are later in the day and my mood could change drastically. I hope for the good of the two men I have a great conversation early in the morning with Shane. I don't want my world to tumble and then to be fake and perform a nice act later. I have written over a numerous of times what I'll say to Shane. I will tell him I love him.

Thursday morning and I am sweating profusely, my sheets are soaked, my hair drenched. Fuck, I can't do this.

"Sky!!" I yell, "Skylar!" again. She comes running in, "What?"

"I need help, I can't do this. I am a heaping sweaty mess. Call Mr. Michaels and cancel for me, please." Half crying, half begging.

"You know I am not going to do something so entirely crazy. Now, get your sorry ass up and tell the man you love him." She nudges me in the side. "Do you know what you are going to wear?"

"No, I don't. See I shouldn't go, I don't even have an outfit picked out." I smile at her in hopes she'll agree. She turns pulling out a jade green V-neck wrap dress. "Perfect, settle but sexy."

"You are supposed to be my friend and help me out, no push me into disaster." I sit up agreeing with her choice of selection. "Alright, I'll go. I'll go and make a huge fool of myself and after I am done we are moving away." Yeah that sounds good, move away. I slowly move my body and attempt to get ready. I look good I must say. The green dress is exactly what sky had said, 'settle but sexy'.

I walk casually to the park no need to rush however I do feel my feet pick up the pace. I find the bench and wait. This is the toughest part, waiting. Ten minutes have gone by and still no Mr. Michaels. This isn't like him, I look at my phone no messages or missed calls. Another ten minutes then fifteen more, he is now forty-five minutes late. My heart sinks, I've been stood up, I am a fool. I stand to leave just as I hear my phone buzz, it's him, Mr. Michaels

> *Please forgive me Precious, an emergency occurred, and I had to rush and attend the matter. May I please make this up to you. Give me a couple of days to arrange this matter, then I am all yours. I want more than nothing to hear how you wish to start the*

next chapter of your journey, new adventures.
Please accept my forgiveness.

Always yours,
Master

I wanted to throw my phone, I wanted to scream. But instead I sat back down and cried. After most the day had gone by I remember I'm meeting Kane and Victor. I am in no mood for them tonight as I knew if this event turned with Shane I would be a complete mess. I walk back home to make myself presentable. I stay in my dress but clean up my face from the tears that left streaks lined down my cheeks. I open my website and emails. I look to find I have an email from Kane. I quickly open it before I shut down the site. I am done, it's completely over.

My Mistress,

I have been thinking long and hard for my reason of heartbreak, of loss, of fear of never having that feeling again in my life. I never wanted the pain that came with love. So, I drove women in and out of my house. I too am a well-known man, so I often wondered if a female could look over the fame and my bank account to love me for me, all of me. Then one day she entered my home and I fell immediately. She was sexy, smart, funny, and caring. She came from being tied down herself, from her fame to people controlling her. She just wanted to escape from all of it.

The moment she left my office the very first day, I knew she would be the death of me and by that, I mean break my heart. I wanted her to stay, I wanted her to stay forever. I knew she needed to leave go explore the world and be free. It was hard to watch her walk away the hardest thing I have ever had to do. She was my Precious and she will always be my Precious.

Yours Always.

Holy Fuck! Is it? It couldn't be. Maybe it is a coincidence but maybe it's not. My palms are clammy, shaking nervously. He didn't sign off, he left it blank. I need to know. So, I type back but only one word.

Master?

Yes, Precious

You have been Kane this whole time? I don't understand. Why didn't you just call or come for me. That guy that I see, in the trench coat, is that you too? Master, I have so many mixed emotions going through my mind, I don't know how to feel right now. I want to kiss you but also kick your ass. Should I be happy or pissed?

Yours forever.
Miranda, I love you

Fuck!

What the hell? What the fucking hell? I can right now, I…. I'm meeting Victor and Kane but not *Kane because Kane is you. Master!*

> *Miranda, Precious, please I have a lot of explaining to do I know this. I can't hold off any longer, please meet Me, your Master tonight. Dan can come pick you up.*

> *I can get there on my own, thank you. I will text you when I am done meeting with Victor I owe him that.*

Wow what a shit show. I can't even digest any of this. I re-read all of it. Kane is Mr. Michaels all along, this while time he has expressing his love for me but as someone else. Mother fucker. It's time to meet Victor. I close my computer and head off.

The place is packed so parking is only open on the side of the road. It's not well lite either and I really dislike that I am completely this stupid to meet a man that first I am a little creeped out from and doing so alone. I manage to get past a few cars before I am swung around with a hand around my throat and a body a very cold, strong body against mine. Colin. Our eyes make contact as he smirks, stay holding tightly with is hand to my throat. His breath warm as he inches closer.

"I told you, you were mine." Out of the blue another voice travels from behind me.

"That's where you are wrong, she is mine." I close my eyes as an object nears my face and the next thing I hear is a thud. I tense as I feel hands reach my face and cup my cheeks.

"It's ok Precious. I got you." I slowly open my eyes to that familiar voice. "Master." I wrap my arms around him and hold tight. I begin to sob uncontrollably as he held me close to his chest. I did take in his scent, I've missed his smell so much. I pull away, looking completely exhausted and frightened I say, "How did you know I was here?"

"Well," he says, "Oh never mind, you are Kane and I was to meet Kane here as well. Why didn't you show up this morning?"

"I'd like to apologize again for missing our time together. I honestly had an emergency to attend. You are so important to me, while I was away you were all I thought about. How incredible ridiculous I am for leaving you there and this was a huge step for you too. For us. I so badly wanted to be with you, please accept my apologies."

"You are forgiven especially after saving my life. Thank you Master."

"You know the cops are going to want to question you and me. Colin has been looking for you for some time as you were aware and for some reason he knew you had a website. Never know how careful you need to be on the internet." We hear the sirens, Dan has called them. Yes, Dan the driver was there as well incase Colin had a weapon and Shane needed help.

We all gave our story to the police, mine was a bit longer being I knew Colin and he was my manager that I had a fall out with. Colin will be doing time back in IL due to all his charges against him there. Mr. Michaels agreed he go back there to be charged. The police all hang about talking amongst each other to piece each of our stories together. I stand against a police vehicle in shock of this evenings event. Shane walks over, wraps his arms around me and holds me close into his chest. Safe and protected. He kisses my forehead, I feel his throat make a clearing as he is ready to speak.

"We need to talk Precious, I believe you know this too. I have much to say and I owe you a huge explanation."

I cry more in his arms. I can't do this not right now. "Shane, I can't. I just want to go home and sleep. I am so exhausted. Not only from Colin being in town but he portrayed to be a sub of mine and you. You did too. I just want to sleep then wake up and make all this come together make an understanding of it all."

"I am right with you. Please allow me to drive you home and if I may, stay." I pull my head back to look him straight in the eyes, he needs to know I am serious, and I am hurting badly at the moment.

"No, Shane. I don't want you to come over. I don't want you to drive me home either. I can manage all one my own." I start to walk away slowly. My mind is a pure mess of emotions. I am waved from the cops to leave, if they have more questions they know how to reach me. Shane follows just an inch behind as I reach my car. He holds he door open for me, then he leans down and calmly says, "I wish you wouldn't be left alone tonight. May I please accompany you to your home?" I can't even look at him, I know I will cave,

"I'm sorry Shane, not tonight I need to be left alone."

"Be safe Precious. I need you safe." With that he closes the door. I watch him through my rearview mirror as I drive off, tears streaming down my face. I feel like a complete fool, like I was lied too and toyed with. I'm feeling angry now than sad and frightened.

I arrive home safe just as Shane wanted. But I didn't say I'd be safe once I enter through the door. Skylar bounced on me immediately. She had called everyone; Brayden, Jake, Stephanie, Taylor, Simon and Simons wife. I want to turn around and leave. I hold my hands up to plea my innocence. "Everyone, I am fine. Yes, Colin was here, yes Colin tried to attack me. Key word tried. I am okay just a lot went was brought to my attention tonight and I need serious relaxing. I start off to my room but stop in my tracks. I turn around to everyone. "Thank you all so much for caring. For coming here and waiting. I appreciate you all so much, but I really need to go relax. I will tell everything once I have had a chance to gather it myself. I turn back on my heels and into my room I go face down into my pillows and sob. I cried for what seemed like hours until I heard my phone go off with a text alert. Shane's name appeared.

> *Precious I am worried; please tell me you have made it home safely? Please say yes to my next question. Will you meet me tomorrow evening at 8pm downtown at the Loon? Please, I need to share a little something I had planned to do for a long time.*

> *I am safe, thank you. Sure, I will meet you tomorrow night. Good night Shane.*

I turn my phone off and close my eyes.

CHAPTER 12

Laying wide awake in bed, I replay the events of yesterday. I start with Mr. Michaels texting me that he is unable to meet for an important matter had taken a priority over me. However, his text didn't come until almost an hour later. I am puzzled, an hour later. What could he have been doing before he had to deal with his important issue? Was he that busy that he couldn't call or text before we were to meet? Did he forget about meeting me? I have so much turning in my head and it's all bad thoughts to his reason of texting me so late into the time we were to meet. It's just not like him. After brain storming about that I went into the email from Kane, well actually from Shane. Finding out it has been him all along. I remember from the beginning when he sent songs that fit so well with the way I felt too. He was expressing himself to me knowing I didn't know and using this form was keeping him safe. He could show his self, his feeling which he has never felt before and which scared him immensely. This way was in his comfort, it was a soft limit which helped him. Then just yesterday he said, "I love you" A tingle spreads throughout my body thinking of his words. I love you too I say out loud in my room.

Thank god he was there last night at the club. Colin would have had me buried somewhere if Shane hadn't shown up. Colin, he too was a sub of mine, stalking me and using me to get closer. This world is messed up. I was so scared looking into Colin's eyes, he was so angry, he wanted revenge badly. I should call my mom. Odd, that just popped into my head. I wonder if she even cares what I am up too or if I am doing well? I thought of her and therefore I should call. Later.

He loves me. I like the way it sounds in my head. Shane Michaels loves Me, Miranda Scott. Just as I am lost in my love moment a knock pounds on my door, then a body storm into my room. Skylar. She plants her body next to mine on the bed.

"Tell me everything. I've waited long enough this morning and I want to know everything." As I am about to answer her another body pops into my room, "Me too." Brayden. I give Sky a smirk and look back at him with a smile.

"Alright but can we do this out in the kitchen I need coffee first." We all gather out to the table while I make another pot of coffee.

"We don't need to wait for the coffee to be done, do we?" Sky snarks, I see Brayden grab her hand to calm her anxious attitude. I smile knowing I put those two together.

"Okay, I can start. My day started with meeting Shane, Mr. Michaels at the park, he didn't show. Well he texted me about an hour into it that he had an emergency and will not be able to attend." My eyes immediately go to Brayden, I wanted to see if he gave off any clues to knowing where Shane was at that time. No, he didn't, bummer. "So, I left

and came here to cry and get ready for my meeting with
Victor. Victor was a sub, like Brayden and since I was ending
my website I thought I owed it to the men that I meet with
them and wish them all the best in their future endeavors.
Victor and I were to gather at the Outlook, I had invited
Kane another sub to join. Victor scared me, he was more
controlling, seemed more alpha wanted the lead rather than
listen to a female give him instructions. This way if Kane
was there I wouldn't be alone nor frightened. While I was
emailing Kane, he began speaking in a different language
a common one he and I talk. We spoke through songs. It
was until he decided to write more and more he did. In
one of his last emails he called the lady in his life, Precious.
That's what Shane calls me. Then he left his sign off open.
I said "Master" and he responded with "yes, Precious" Kane
has been Shane as well. I feel completely deceived. Most
importantly Shane told me he loves me." I smile big. "He
saved me from Colin. So, I still went to the Outlook where
I was going to introduce myself to Victor but then ended up
being attacked by Colin. Before he could even lay a hand on
me Shane arrived and put Colin in his place. Dan, Shane's
driver called the cops and Colin is back in IL with charges
going against him there and the ones here against me. Shane
wants me to meet up with him to night at the Loon." I shrug
my shoulders, I don't know. "I might go but I just can't deal
with all this right now you know? I want to be wrapped up
so badly in his arms, but I also am disgusted by his sneaky
ways to reach out to me. I need more time to think about
it." I look at the two of them, I see everything that I have
just said is still digesting. I get up to leave.

"Are you okay Miranda?" Brayden kindly asks.

"Yeah, I'll be alright. Thank you."

"Anytime sweetheart," he replies, Sky smiles at him then turns to me, "I think you should go tonight. I have this feeling it'll be good if you do. He, Mr. Michaels needs this, he needs to show you how he feels, and he needs to express it out of his comfort zone. Therefore, he asked you to go to the Loon, it'll be busy, and he is going to do something grand. I feel it."

"Grand or not, I do need to clear all this up. A talk with the man I have been loving for so long might be the cure I need. I will go only if you two don't follow me." I point my finger at them both. Brayden puts his hands up and surrenders, Sky shrugs her shoulders, "maybe." She says. I point at her with a mean glare, then turn to go back to bed.

I didn't fall asleep. I re read mine and master's last emails, the one where he basically tells me who he is. Bits and piece leave a trace my mind. Fuck!

> *I wanted her to stay, I wanted her to stay forever. I knew she needed to leave go explore the world and be free. It was hard to watch her walk away the hardest thing I have ever had to do. She was my Precious and she will always be my Precious.*
>
> *Master?*
>
> *Yes, Precious*
>
> *Miranda, I love you*

I say to myself in my room, I love you Shane Michaels, I always have. I pick up my phone I want to call him but instead I text.

> *Hi, it's me, Miranda. I just wanted to reach out, let you know I am doing good today. I spoke with Skylar and Brayden, they are a couple now. I keep reading over our last messages where I think you are Kane. I kept a list of all the songs you wished for me to listen too when you were trying to speak your love language to me as Kane. I love you Shane but there is something telling me to hold back, for now anyways. I do plane to see you tonight at the Loon around 8pm as you had stated. I am very much looking forward to our chat, iron out the wrinkles.*
>
> *I will see you later.*

Proof read it and press send. Pleased with my text I relax. What am I going to say tonight, I guess just listen to him speak first then decide how to respond. He loves me. That's a feeling I never want to lose. My buzzes.

> *My darling Precious*
>
> *Thank you for sending the message of your wellbeing. Consciously I did want to know you were well. You haven't left my mind, I've thought about you all night. I hope you can stand my tired, droopy face tonight. I*

> *too am looking forward to explaining it all,*
> *openly and honestly. Miranda, I am sorry for*
> *frustration, for confusion, for pain and heart*
> *ache. I love you Miranda and I want to speak*
> *these words every day, I want to show you*
> *every day.*

> *I'll see you tonight My sweet Precious*

I get so giddy and excited when I hear from him, even if it's a little text. I love the way he makes me feel, best feeling in the world. I dig through my closet, decisions on what outfit I should wear tonight. I will dress casual but classy. I find a pair of dark skinny jeans and a silk fuscia colored blouse cut off at the sleeves, and my tan belt with matching tan strapped heeled sandals. My hair, I have no idea what to do with it, if it lays right then I'll leave it done otherwise it'll go up. I still have a few hours before I need to get ready, so I go down to the café and I bring some of my sketches. Beautiful day to take a walk so I decide to go the long way around town, gather thoughts before my night happens. I have a sense I am being watched and yet there he is, my trench coat stalker. Since knowing that Colin is in town I figured it to be him even though the build did not fit. If not him I did think it was Shane, the figure has similar features just as far from height, and build. Otherwise, I have not been close enough to see this person's face. I add a little speed to my pace. Turning the corner, I look back and they are gone. Another day I have made it safe with the trench coat stalker.

I can't seem to keep my concentration, my focus is on him, Shane, My Master. I should be creating a fall line for Rose n Main. Simon will not be happy with me if I do another rush on fabric like I did for the show. I go back to my drawings. I notice I am doodling the words he loves me. I smile I love you too I say in my thoughts. Time flew while I got lost in Shane and my love for him. I packed up my belongings and took the short way home this time.

I grab a cab and tell him "The Loon downtown." My stomach is twisted in knots, I'm starting to feel warm. I pay the cab driver and head into the bar. The place is backed just as Sky had stated. I look everywhere for Shane and even walk the place a couple times. I stand at the front hostess desk, I asked if she remembers Shane Michaels entering, she tells me she just started and didn't see any one of that I am explaining come in. I text him, nothing. I am about to leave when I hear over the loud speaker,

"Miranda, stay." I pause at that word. That one word could have and can change my life for the better. A hand touches my shoulder, "Miranda, please don't leave. I have so much to say, to explain. I need this tonight, I need us to understand each other and I need you to hear me out. I should have told you to stay the moment you said you had to leave. I never wanted you to go but I couldn't force volume from my vocal cords to rise out of my pounding chest. I was in so much pain, fear mostly." He drags his hands through his thick dark hair, "Miranda, my life shattered when that door closed behind you. I thought by letting you go was the smart choice, but it destroyed us both, well I'll speak for myself, but I do believe you wanted to stay too." He cups my face, his beautiful blue eyes take a serious but generous hold to mine, "I need you in my life, Miranda. You are living in my heart, you consume my daily thoughts, your passion flows through my veins. Stay Miranda, stay with me. I love you." I am completely numb, my body can't move, I can't make out a sound. I just stand there like a frozen statue looking into his beautiful eyes. "I see all this is a lot to absorb, a bit overwhelming. I have more, and this is, as you know way out of my comfort zone, but you do this to me, you make me feel alive. I have been practicing a song. I'm going to sing it after all it is karaoke night. Listen to the words Precious, they are for you." With that he kisses my cheek and heads back up to the stage.

A song starts to play, Aerosmith; Angel. Then Shane walks onto the stage holding a microphone. He looks sexy as hell right now. He begins to sing, himself, his voice in front of everyone in this club. His voice is amazing, he sounds close to Aerosmith. A smile cracks at the side of my mouth for I wonder how long he has been working on this? I hear; *the crying that I do is for you, I want your love. Let's break the walls between us.* Gerd, that line is so true. We both have had our walls up, afraid of letting our feelings go for sake of being denied, unwanted. He's suffered and seen the light, I've suffered all this time too. I'm his angel and he needs saving, here I am. I am here tonight but I need saving too. I feel wet warm tears slide down my cheeks as he sings loneliness took him for a ride. He is nothing without my love. Now he has gotten down on his knees singing to me now, fuck he is perfect. Again, he sings come and save me tonight. There's a lyric break as he walks to the end of the stage reaches one hand out, points at me in the crowd, and starts to sing again

You're the reason I live

You're the reason I die

You're the reason I give when I break down and cry

That's exactly what Brayden told me, he has seen Shane break down and cry, act off and oddly since my departure. He has everyone's attention here in the bar. He holds enormous amounts of power but right now, however only he and I know he is at his weakest moment. I continue to watch and take in every word he is singing, our eyes are clued, memorized by the love we hold for each other but also terrified for the strength it holds. The song comes to an end as he hands the microphone to the karaoke member and walks towards me. The entire place is going wild with applause and screams. I can't help but to smile, cry, laugh, and clap myself. All he has to do is walk straight his sexy ass to me with that smirk holding back his embarrassment, as he stands tall and confident.

"Miranda, I love you. I can't live without you, I've tried, and it isn't working. Please come back to me. Let it be just us, you and me." He swipes the tears from under my eyes with his thumb. Waiting for a response, we hold our stare looking deep into each other's soul. "Precious?"

He says in a question.

"I love you too Shane, but I'm scared."

"Precious please don't be scared. I experienced that feeling as well and it drove me to insanity, to almost losing you. I never felt love before, I have never wanted love and here I am confessing all my love to you, Miranda. I can't watch you leave again." He takes me into his arms, this is where I am meant to be.

"We have so much to talk about but yes, Master, I want to be yours forever."

"Always," he finishes it. We walk out of the bar his arm around my shoulders and mine around his waist, he kisses me gently on the temple. Another loud applause happens for us, the bar cheers for us. Dan is waiting for us outside with the car.

"Good evening Mr. Michaels. Very pleased to see you Miss Scott." He smiles broadly.

"It's always wonderful to see you Dan," I say in return, placing a kiss on his cheek. I have always enjoyed Dan even when he first thought I was another one-off Master's ladies. Shane stepping aside as Dan holds the car door open, "Ladies first," he says, "Dan" he says with a nod, that's Shane responding to good evening. Shane holds me in his arms the entire way home. He whispers in my ear, "I should really punish you for being so difficult," I open my mouth ready to defend myself, but he holds up his finger to silence me, "however, I have been too. So, I think tonight calls for lots of make-up sex instead of punishments." He turns towards me no to hear my thoughts on tonight's events.

"I agree Master. No punishments, we both have been difficult dealing with our feelings in different ways. We both thought the other wanted something else, yet we never stop to think perhaps it was the same. I love the idea of makeup sex or love making tonight. Don't forget we also need to have more of a conversation as to what we both want. We love each other but I need to know is it us? You and me? Or does your Master and subs still exist? Are we going to continue this lifestyle? There is so much going on inside my head Master."

"Easy Precious. First, I want you, in my bed naked. I want to cherish your beautiful body with me lips, eyes, and hands. I want to explore you're the spots the drive you crazy, I want to hear your moans of ecstasy, I want to devour you needs and caress your cravings. I'll make all your dreams come true tonight if you allow me this, Precious. Then, we can have our conversation, I already know how it will end." He winks at me as if no matter what I say he will get what he wants. However, he does have my body aching, throbbing for his touch. I grab his face pull towards my lips and just before I kiss him passionately I stop centimeter away, allow my warm breath out as I whisper, "I love you Shane Michaels," then I kiss him so deep he fills the desire throughout his body, leaving chills in the wake. I graze my hand over his manhood, his cock has doubled in size and I couldn't be more pleased with myself.

"Why the smile Precious. You enjoying the outcome of your kiss?"

"Indeed, I am Master." Now arriving at the manor, Dan opens the back door for us to exit. Taking my hand, he leads me into the house and straight to his room, the Masters room. There he closes the door, turns with a devilish grin across his face as I see him undressing me with just his look. He is a man that can have you orgasm with just his look and I can feel the heat begin between my legs. He walks towards me, "you look beautiful tonight," he says, "you always look beautiful," he finishes. He goes straight to my neck with soft kisses while his hand works pulling my clothing items off. As smooth as possible he unattached my bra, my ladies bounce perky, eager to be sucked as he so invitingly takes them in his mouth. My head falls back in pure bliss, I haven't been touched since the last time I have been in my Masters arms. I allow him to take me, to control the situation. He likes the lead and I will allow him his happiness. He follows his kisses down my belly, where he slides his hands into my pants and magically makes them disappear. I can't help but to smile, this where I belong, with my Master.

After a fabulous night of mind blowing love making and talking, we have come to an understanding. This is where he wants me to be, in his Manor with him always. I agreed. I just want to be surrounded by the man I love and be cherished in return. This will not be easy for the both of us, but relationships aren't easy. He and I are both difficult in our own ways and I do love tending to his babyish manner. He loves to discipline me, and I am learning from it which in hand turns out to be a good lesson to the both of us. I am me and I have no filters here, he comes with passion that I embrace fully. Our love is unlimited for each other, I only see this as my future, I see him in my future and that warms me deeply.

"I see that smile across your face Precious, what thoughts are traveling in your beautiful mind that places such a lovely picture?" I turn looking at him, "Us, you, everything. I look ahead and I see us. This is what causes a smile across my face, Master." He pulls me into his chest and squeezes me tight, "I love you Precious. You are my world, my light, my forever." I kiss his cheek and reply, "Always." We laid in bed holding each other for a long time until both our tummies rumbled. "How about we get some breakfast, plus I believe you have a lot of texts you'll need to reply too." I watch as he rolls out of bed and admire his backside. This man is beautiful, and he is mine. I did just as he suggested I checked my text messages. Oh, mer gerd, Sky left about a hundred, Simon, and Jack did too. Oh geez, I am scared to call so I decide texting is safer. I text Simon first, letting him know I am fine, happy and safe. Now, Jake, I text the same except I add that I am with Mr. Michaels. Finally, Sky, after I text her my phone starts ringing. Nervously I answer,

"Hello"

"What the fuck Miranda?" I hold the phone away from my ear since she's yelling. I look over at Shane to see if he heard thankfully he didn't react, so I guess that's a no.

"Yes."

"What the fuck?" She says again. I chuckle, "so you think this is funny? I almost called the cops Miranda, this isn't funny."

"Clearly you knew I was fine since you didn't call the cops."

"Are you getting smart with me Miranda? Luckily, I had Brayden here and he texted Shane for me, in which Shane responded, unlike you."

"I am so sorry, Sky believe me. All this is just so messed up, but I know now at least I know, he has loved me too, all this time we were fools wanting each other but thinking the other didn't want us. I can't even swallow all this, it's being processed but hard to imagine. Me, Mr. Michaels loves me."

"Why is that so hard to believe Miranda? You are, someone to love and who ever receives your love back is very lucky."

"She's right you know," A sexy voice from behind me says

"Master, you snoopy in on my conversation?" My face beat red and my heart filled with pride. He leans down kisses my head, "tell her you'll see her later, I drew us a bath and then we are going to go get your belongings because I want you here with me all the damn time." He takes my hand and leads the way to the bathroom. I quickly text Sky.

"Must go, Master wants to play. I'll see you later."

"Have fun sweetie," say replies and I toss the phone down.

Holding my hand, he helps me climb over the side of the tub, then he climbs in behind me. Laying back in his arms bubbles pop around us, I nestle my head against his chest.

"I love you Precious Always."

"I love you too Master, forever."

THE END

Printed in the United States
By Bookmasters